This book may be kept

# THE DESERTED HOUSE

# THE
# DESERTED
# HOUSE

Lydia Chukovskaya

TRANSLATED BY ALINE B. WERTH

New York      E. P. Dutton & Co., Inc.

26, 121

THE HERO OF MY STORY, WHOM I LOVE WITH ALL MY HEART, WHOM I HAVE TRIED TO RECREATE IN ALL HIS BEAUTY, AND WHO WAS, IS AND WILL FOREVER BE BEAUTIFUL IS—TRUTH.

—L. N. Tolstoy

This story was written twenty-two years ago, in Leningrad, in the winter of 1939–1940. In it I attempted to record the events just experienced by my country, my friends and myself. I could not refrain from writing about them, though I had, of course, no hope at the time of seeing this story in print. I had little hope even that the school exercise book containing the clean copy of it would escape destruction and be preserved. To keep it in the drawer of my desk was dangerous, but to burn it was more than I could bring myself to do. I regarded it not so much as a story as a piece of evidence, which it would be dishonorable to destroy.

The war came. The siege of Leningrad began and ended. The people keeping the manuscript perished, but the manuscript itself survived. Having left Leningrad a month before the war began, I spent the years 1941–1944 far away from my native city; and it was only at the end of the war that my exercise book, after a long absence, miraculously found its way back into my hands.

The war ended. Stalin died. My hitherto unrealizable hopes that the time was drawing near when the story would see the light of day steadily grew.

After the speeches made at the XXth and XXIInd Party Congresses, pointing to a better present and denouncing the darker aspects of the past, I became more anxious than ever that my story should be made available to readers and so serve to further a cause which I regard as vitally important: in the name of the future, to help to reveal the causes and the consequences of the great tragedy the people had suffered.

I do not doubt that literary works describing the thirties will abound, and that other writers, in possession of far more facts than I myself at that time possessed, besides greater literary gifts and greater powers of analysis, will give a more complete and comprehensive picture of this period. I have merely tried, to the best of my ability, to record what I personally observed.

But however great the merits of any future tales or accounts may be, they will all have been written at another period, separated from 1937 by decades; whereas my story was written with the impression of events still fresh in my mind. Herein lies the difference between my story and any others which will be devoted to the years 1937–1938. Herein, I consider, lies its claim to the reader's attention.

It is for this reason that I now refrain from making any changes in it, beyond omitting an introductory passage which today seems irrelevant. May it speak today as a voice from the past, the tale of a witness striving conscientiously, against the powerful forces of falsehood, to discern and record the events occurring before his eyes.

# THE DESERTED HOUSE

## ONE

After the death of her husband, Olga Petrovna took a course in typing. She felt she simply had to acquire a profession: it would be a long time yet before Kolya began to earn. After he got through school he must, whatever happened, take the examination for admission to an institute—Fyodor Ivanovich would never have allowed his son to remain without a higher education.

Olga Petrovna mastered the typewriter easily; but then, she was much more literate than all these modern young ladies. Having received the highest skill rating on her certificate, she soon found herself a job in one of the big Leningrad publishing houses.

She became completely absorbed in the office routines. After a month of it, she simply couldn't understand how she had ever lived without office work. True, it was unpleasant getting up in the cold of the morning by electric light, and it was shivering cold waiting for the streetcar in a crowd of sleepy, scowling people. True, the clatter of the typewriters gave her a headache toward the end of the working day. But that didn't matter—how fascinating, how interesting, working turned out to be! As a little girl she had loved going to school and used to weep when they kept her at home with a cold, and now she loved going to the office.

Seeing that she was conscientious and discreet, they soon made her senior typist—in charge of the typing pool so to speak. It was her job to assign the work, count pages and lines and clip the sheets together—and Olga Petrovna liked all this much better than doing the typing herself. Whenever there was a knock on the window she opened the wooden shutter and took in the papers with quiet dignity, and without a waste of words. Most of them were accounts, plans, reports, official letters and orders, but now and again there would be a manuscript from some contemporary writer.

"It will be ready in twenty-five minutes," Olga Petrovna would say, glancing at the clock on the wall, "precisely."

And if anyone tried to object, saying that it was urgent, and he had to have it sooner, she would interrupt in midsentence:

"—No, in exactly twenty-five minutes and no sooner!" —and she would slam the window to prevent further argument.

She thought a moment, then gave the work to the typist she felt was most suitable for the particular job—if a document was brought by the director's secretary, it went to the girl who was fastest, most literate and most accurate.

12

In her youth there had been days when she was lonely, days when Fyodor Ivanovich—a doctor with a large practice—was away for long periods visiting his patients, and she had dreamed of having her own dressmaking shop: a large, light room, with pretty girls sitting bent over billowing lengths of silk, and herself showing them the styles and engaging in social conversation with elegant ladies when they came for fittings.

But the typing pool was even better, more important somehow. Now Olga Petrovna was often the first person to read a new work of Soviet literature, some story or novel, while it was still only in manuscript form; and although Soviet stories and novels seemed boring to her—there was such a lot about battles and tractors and factory shops and hardly anything about love—she couldn't help being flattered.

She began to curl her hair, which had turned gray early, and when washing it she added a little blueing to the water to keep it from yellowing. In her simple black work smock—relieved by a little collar of genuine old handmade lace—with a carefully sharpened pencil sticking out of the breast pocket, she felt she looked elegant as well as businesslike and efficient.

The typists were a bit afraid of her, and called her the schoolmarm behind her back. But they obeyed her. And she wanted to be strict, but fair. In the lunch hour she chatted in a friendly way with those who did their work well and conscientiously, talked about how difficult it was to make out the director's handwriting and how lipstick was far from suitable for everyone. But with those who were capable of typing things like "rehersal" or "collictive" she adopted a haughty manner.

One of the typists, Zoya Viktorovna, really got on Olga

Petrovna's nerves: she made a mistake in almost every word, smoked in an insolent manner and chattered all the time she was working. She reminded Olga Petrovna vaguely of a fresh housemaid they had once employed in the old days. The maid's name was Fanny, and she had been rude to Olga Petrovna and flirted with Fyodor Ivanovich . . . what's the point of keeping anyone like that!

Of all the typists in the pool, the one Olga Petrovna liked best was Natasha Frolenko, a modest, rather plain girl with a drab complexion. She never made any mistakes in her typing, and she always did her margins and paragraphing beautifully. Her work looked as if it was done on some special paper and with a better typewriter than the others used. Although in fact both the paper and the typewriter Natasha used were no different from the others, and the whole secret—come to think of it—lay in her accuracy.

The typing pool was separated from the rest of the building by a door in which there was a little window, covered by a small brown-varnished wooden shutter. The door was always kept locked, and all conversations took place through the window.

At the beginning, Olga Petrovna knew no one in the publishing house except her own typists and the messenger woman who carried the documents. But gradually she got to know everyone there.

Some two weeks had passed since she took the job, but already an accountant, a sedate, bald but young-looking man, was coming up to chat with Olga Petrovna in the corridor. He had recognized her—some twenty years ago, Fyodor Ivanovich had treated him very successfully when he was ill. The accountant was fond of boating and Western European dancing, and Olga Petrovna was pleased that he asked her to join their dance club.

The director's secretary, an elderly and well-mannered lady, began to say good morning to her, the head of personnel bowed to her, so did a well-known writer, a handsome, gray-haired man who wore a beaver cap and carried a monogrammed brief case, and always arrived at the publisher's in his own car.

The writer even asked her one day how she liked the last chapter of his novel. "We literary people noticed long ago that typists are the fairest judges. It's true," he said with a smile, showing his even set of false teeth. "They judge a thing spontaneously, they are not affected by preconceived ideas like the comrade critics or editors."

Olga Petrovna also became acquainted with the Party organizer, Timofeyev, a lame, unshaven man. He was sullen, looked down at the floor when speaking, and Olga Petrovna was a little afraid of him. Occasionally he would appear at the window with the assistant manager, and ask for Zoya Viktorovna; then Olga Petrovna would unlock the door and the assistant manager would drag Zoya Viktorovna's typewriter out of the typing pool into the restricted special department, Zoya Viktorovna following with a triumphant expression. As it was explained to Olga Petrovna, Zoya Viktorovna had been "security cleared," and the Party organizer summoned her to the special department to type out secret Party documents.

Soon Olga Petrovna knew everyone in the publishing house—their names, their jobs and what they looked like —ledger clerks, editors, technical editors, messengers.

At the end of her first month at the office, she saw the director for the first time. The director's office had a thick carpet on the floor, around the table were deep, soft armchairs, and on the table three whole telephones. The director turned out to be a young man, not over thirty-five;

15

tall, well-shaven, wearing an elegant gray suit with three badges, and a fountain pen in his hand. He spoke to Olga Petrovna for two minutes or so, but even during those two minutes the telephone rang three times and as he spoke into one telephone, he lifted the receiver off another. The director himself pushed up a chair for her and asked politely whether she would be so kind as to stay on late that evening to do some overtime work. She could choose any typist she liked and dictate a report to her. "I am told that you are very good at making out my atrocious writing," he said with a smile.

Olga Petrovna left his office with a feeling of pride in his authority and flattered by his confidence in her. A well-brought-up young man. They said that he was an ordinary worker who had made his way up—and indeed, his hands looked rough, but apart from that . . .

At the first general meeting of the workers of the publishing firm which she attended, Olga Petrovna was bored. The director made a short speech about the rise to power of the German fascists, and the burning of the Reichstag in Germany, and then drove away in his Ford. Then came a speech by the Party organizer, Comrade Timofeyev. He paused so long between two sentences that one thought he had finished. He was followed by the chairman of the Mestkom,* a stout lady wearing a cameo on her bosom. Rubbing and twisting her long fingers, she announced that, in view of all the events, it was first of all essential to tighten up on working hours and wage a relentless campaign against tardiness. She then went on to make a short statement in a hysterical voice about Thaelmann, and proposed that all workers should join the MOPR.† Olga

* Local trade union committee—Translator.
† International Aid to Revolutionaries Organization—Translator.

Petrovna wasn't very clear what it was all about; she was bored, and would have liked to leave, but was afraid that wouldn't be the thing to do, and glared at one of the typists who was making her way toward the door.

However, soon even these meetings ceased to bore Olga Petrovna. At one of these, the director, reporting on the fulfillment of the plan, said that the attainment of the high output figures which must be achieved depended on conscientious, disciplined work by every member of the collective—and not only on the conscientiousness of editors and authors, but also of the cleaning woman and the messenger, and of each individual typist. "Incidentally," he said, "I would like to say that the work of the typing office, under the supervision of Comrade Lipatova, has already attained an exceptionally high standard."

Olga Petrovna blushed and it was a long time before she dared to raise her eyes again. When she did at last decide to look around, she thought how kind and nice everyone looked, and found all the statistics unexpectedly interesting.

All her free time Olga Petrovna now spent with Natasha Frolenko.

But she had less and less free time. Overtime work or, more often, meetings of the Mestkom, of which Olga Petrovna was soon made a member, now took up nearly every evening. More and more often Kolya was left to heat up his dinner himself, and he began to call her, teasingly, his "social-minded mother."

The Mestkom gave her the job of collecting the union dues. Olga Petrovna gave little thought to the reasons why the trade union actually existed, but it pleased her to draw lines on sheets of paper with a ruler and mark in the various columns who had paid their dues for the current month and who had not; it pleased her to paste in the stamps and present impeccable accounts to the auditing commission. It pleased her to be in a position to walk into the director's imposing office whenever she chose and remind him jokingly that he was four months in arrears, to hear him jokingly present his apologies to the patient comrades on the Mestkom, and watch him pull out his wallet and pay up. Even the sullen Party organizer could safely be reminded that he owed his dues.

At the end of her first year at the office, an important event occurred in Olga Petrovna's life: she spoke on behalf of the non-Party employees of the publishing house at the general meeting of the workers.

It happened like this. The publishing house was expecting a visit from some important comrades from Moscow. The assistant manager, a dashing fellow with meticulously parted hair, ran around the publishing house for days dragging some kind of frames on his own back, and sent the floor polishers into the typing pool office just when it was most inconvenient. In the midst of all this commotion, the sullen Party organizer came up to Olga Petrovna in the corridor. "The Party organization, in conjunction with the Mestkom," he said, looking down at the floor as usual, "is going to ask you . . . to make the pledges on behalf of the non-Party activists."

On the eve of the arrival of the visitors from Moscow there was a mass of work to be done. The pool was kept busy typing all sorts of accounts and plans. Practically every evening Olga Petrovna stayed late with Natasha for overtime work. The clatter of the typewriters echoed in the empty room, and the corridors and offices all around were in darkness.

Olga Petrovna liked these evenings. After finishing work, she and Natasha talked for ages, sitting at their typewriters, before going out into the darkness of the corridor. Natasha didn't say much, but was a wonderful listener. "Have you noticed that Anna Grigorievna [she was the chairman of the Mestkom] always has dirty nails?" Olga Petrovna would say. "And yet she wears a cameo, and waves her hair. She'd do better to wash her hands cleaner. . . . Zoya Viktorovna gets on my nerves terribly. She's so insolent. . . . And have you noticed, Natasha, that Anna Grigorievna is always somehow ironical in speaking about the Party organizer? She doesn't like him. . . ."

After talking about the chairman of the Mestkom and the Party organizer, Olga Petrovna told Natasha about her life with Fyodor Ivanovich and how Kolya fell under the tub when he was six months old, and what a pretty little boy he was; everyone turned around in the street to look at him. He was dressed all in white, a white cape and a white hood. . . .

Natasha somehow seemed to have nothing to tell—not a single romance. "Of course, with a complexion like that . . ." Olga Petrovna thought to herself. Natasha had had nothing but unpleasantness in her life. Her father, a colonel, had died in 1917 of a heart attack—Natasha was barely five at the time. Their house had been taken away from them, and they had to go to live with some relative who was paralyzed. Natasha's mother was a spoiled, helpless woman. They suffered badly from hunger and Natasha had gone to work when she was not more than fifteen. Now Natasha was completely alone; her mother had died the year before last of tuberculosis, her relatives of old age. Natasha was in sympathy with the Soviet regime, but when she had applied for Komsomol membership she had been turned down.

"My father was a colonel and houseowner and, you see, they don't believe that I can sincerely sympathize with the

21

regime," explained Natasha with a frown. "And perhaps they're right, from the Marxist point of view."

She flushed whenever she talked about being refused by the Komsomol, and Olga Petrovna would hurriedly change the subject.

The important day arrived. The portraits of Lenin and Stalin were put into new frames which the assistant manager himself brought and the director's desk was covered with red cloth. The Moscow visitors—two stout men wearing foreign-made suits and ties, and with foreign fountain pens clipped in their breast pockets—were sitting at the table with the director, under the portraits of Lenin and Stalin, and taking papers out of their bulging foreign-made brief cases. Next to them the Party organizer, in his Russian shirt and jacket, looked very insignificant. The dashing assistant manager and the elevator woman, Marya Karpovna, bustled around carrying trays with tea, sandwiches and fruit, which they offered first to the visitors and the director, and then afterward to the rest.

Olga Petrovna was so exited that she was unable to listen to the speeches. As though in a trance, she kept her eyes fixed on the water shimmering in the decanter. At a word from the chairman, she went up to the table, turned first toward the director and his guests and then to the meeting, and finally stood facing sideways, hands clasped at the waist, as she had been taught to do as a child when reciting greetings in French verse.

"On behalf of the non-Party workers—" she began in a trembling voice, and then went on with the whole pledge to increase labor productivity, everything she and Natasha had composed together, and which she had learned by heart.

When she came home, she didn't get to bed for a long time, but waited for Kolya to tell him about the meeting.

22

Kolya was taking his final school examinations and spent every evening at Alik Finkelstein's. Alik was his best friend, and they studied together.

Olga Petrovna tidied up the room a little and then went into the kitchen to light the primus stove.

"What a pity that you don't have a job," she said to a co-inhabitant of the apartment who was washing dishes, a good-natured woman married to a policeman. "So many experiences, many new things in life. Especially when your work has to do with literature."

At last Kolya appeared, hungry and soaked through by the first spring rain, and Olga Petrovna placed a plate of cabbage soup before him. She leaned with her elbows on the table opposite Kolya, watching him eat, and was just about to tell him about the speech she had made when he spoke first:

"You know, Mama," he announced proudly, "I am now a Komsomol member. The bureau approved my application today."

Having told this news, he immediately went on to something else, stuffing his mouth full of bread—there had been a row at school.

"Pashka Gusev—he's a real old-regime jerk . . ."

"Kolya, I don't like you using coarse language," Olga Petrovna broke in.

"But that's not the point: Pashka Gusev called Alik Finkelstein a Yid. We decided today at the cell meeting to hold a comrades' court show-trial. And you know who's been appointed as public prosecutor? Me!"

Directly he'd finished eating, Kolya went to bed, and Olga Petrovna also lay down in bed, behind the screen; and Kolya, lying there in the dark, recited Mayakovsky to her by heart.

"The man's a genius, right, Mama?"

And when he had finished Olga Petrovna told him at last about the meeting.

"You're doing fine, Mama," Kolya said, and promptly fell asleep.

## THREE

K olya finished school, the sweltering summer came, and still Olga Petrovna was not given leave. She had to wait until the end of July. She didn't intend to go away anywhere, but she had been eagerly dreaming all through July of how she would be able to sleep late in the mornings, and how she would at last do all the housework which she hadn't had time for because of the demands of the office. She dreamed of getting away from the clatter of the typewriters, of how she would call a painter to repaint the door, of going to look for a topcoat for Kolya and mending his socks; and she simply must go to the cemetery to visit her husband's grave.

But when the vacation days came she discovered that resting is pleasant only on the first day away from work. Accustomed to working, Olga Petrovna continued waking up no later than eight; the painter had finished the door in half an hour; she bought a coat right away for Kolya; in two evenings she had mended all the socks; Fyodor Ivanovich's grave was in perfect order. . . . And the long, empty days dragged on, to the ticking of the clock, with conversations in the kitchen and waiting for Kolya to come home for dinner.

Kolya now spent whole days in the library; he and Alik were studying together for admission to a higher education establishment, the engineering institute, and Olga Petrovna hardly ever saw him. Occasionally she had a visit from Natasha Frolenko, looking tired (she was replacing Olga Petrovna at the office); and Olga Petrovna would eagerly ask her about the director's secretary, the quarrel between the chairman of the Mestkom and the Party organizer, and Zoya Viktorovna's spelling mistakes. And about the discussion held in the director's office about the novel by that nice writer. The entire editorial section had gathered there. . . . "Is it possible that anyone could not like it?" exclaimed Olga Petrovna, clasping her hands. "It gives such a beautiful description of pure first love. Just like Fyodor Ivanovich and me."

Now Olga Petrovna simply couldn't understand at all how she had ever lived without having a job. She absolutely agreed with Kolya when he expounded on it being essential for women to perform socially useful work. And indeed, everything Kolya said and everything they wrote in the papers now seemed to her to be perfectly natural, just as if people had always talked and written like that.

The only thing Olga Petrovna did regret very much, now that Kolya was grown up, was her old apartment. Other people had been moved in a long time ago, during the famine years, right at the beginning of the Revolution.

Fyodor Ivanovich's former office had been taken over by the family of the policeman, Doroshko; an accountant's family was moved into the dining room, and Olga Petrovna and Kolya were left in Kolya's old nursery. Now Kolya was grown up, and it was essential that he should have a room of his own; after all he was no longer a child.

"But, Mama, it wouldn't be fair for Doroshko and his children to live in the cellar, would it? While we lived in a nice apartment? Would that be fair? Tell me!" Kolya would ask severely, and explain to Olga Petrovna the revolutionary significance of filling up the bourgeois flats with extra tenants.

And Olga Petrovna was forced to agree with him; it was true it was not quite fair. Only it was too bad that the policeman's wife was such a slut that the sour smell from her room even filtered out into the corridor. She was scared to death of opening the window vent even a crack. Her twins were already over fifteen, but they still made spelling mistakes.

Olga Petrovna had a new title as consolation for the loss of her apartment: the tenants elected her unanimously as the official representative of the apartment. She thus became, as it were, the boss, the manager of her own apartment. She spoke to the accountant's wife, gently but persistently, about the trunks standing in the corridor. She figured how much each person owed for electricity with the same accuracy as she collected the Mestkom dues at the office. She regularly attended the meetings of official apartment representatives at the dwelling and rent cooperative association, and then gave the inhabitants a detailed report of what the house manager had said.

On the whole, she was on good terms with the other residents of the apartment. When the policeman's wife made jam she would always call Olga Petrovna into the kitchen to taste and see whether she had put enough sugar in. And she often came into Olga Petrovna's room to ask Kolya's advice: what could she do to make sure that the twins would "for God's sake" not stay behind again at school this year—once was enough, heaven knows! And gossip with Olga Petrovna about the accountant's wife, who was a nurse.

"Just try falling into the hands of a nurse like that—she'll have you in the next world before you know it!" declared the policeman's wife emphatically.

The accountant himself was an elderly man with flabby cheeks and blue veins showing on his hands and nose. He was scared of his wife and daughter, and was never heard in the apartment.

But Valya, the accountant's red-haired daughter, shocked Olga Petrovna by the disrespectful way she talked about her mother: "I'll just show her!", "I don't give a damn!" It was true, of course, that Valya's mother was an awful woman. She would stand by her primus stove with a stony expression on her face, and keep nagging at the policeman's wife because her oil stove was smoking, or at the timid twins for not fastening the hook on the door when they got in last at night.

She came of the gentry, she used to spray the corridor with an atomizer of Eau de Cologne, wore trinkets dangling on a chain and spoke in a soft voice, hardly moving her lips, but the words she used were surprisingly coarse.

On paydays Valya would begin to wheedle her mother for money for new shoes. . . . "Don't even think about it, you horse," her mother would say in her flat voice, and Olga Petrovna, so as not to hear what came next, would hurriedly shut herself in the bathroom. But it would not be long before Valya came running in to wash her swollen tear-stained face, pouring into the washbasin all the insults she dared not hurl at her mother to her face.

On the whole, though, apartment forty-six was a pleasant, peaceful one—nothing like number fifty-two right above it, where there was slaughter almost every week on payday. Doroshoko, sleepy after coming off duty, was summoned up there regularly, together with the janitor and the house manager, to draw up a report.

Her vacation dragged on and on. She spent it between the kitchen and her own room, and it finally came to an end, to Olga Petrovna's great joy. The rains had set in, the summer garden was strewn with yellow leaves, trodden into the mud—and Olga Petrovna, in galoshes, umbrella in hand, was again going to the office every day, waiting for the streetcar in the mornings and, at ten o'clock sharp, hanging her number card up on the attendance board with a sigh of relief.

Once again she was surrounded by the clatter and clanging of typewriters, the rustling and crackling of paper, the click of the window opening and shutting. Solemnly Olga Petrovna handed the director's secretary the carefully sorted pages, clipped together and smelling of carbon paper. She pasted stamps into the trade union membership books, sat in on Mestkom meetings to deal with the tightening up of work discipline or the case of some typist or other who had behaved impolitely toward one of the messenger women. She was still a little afraid of the sullen Party organizer, Comrade Timofeyev. She still disliked the chairman of the Mestkom with her dirty nails, secretly adored the director and envied his secretary—but she felt at home with all these people now, they were familiar to her, she felt she belonged there, was confident, and would reproach the insolent Zoya Viktorovna without being shy about it. Indeed, why was she kept on? The matter would have to be raised with the Mestkom.

Kolya and Alik passed the examination for admission to the engineering institute. Seeing their names up on the list of the accepted, they decided to celebrate by setting up a radio set in the apartment. Olga Petrovna did not like it when Kolya and Alik embarked on technical constructions in her room, but she hoped very much that the radio set would cost her less than the ice boat of not long ago. On finishing school, Kolya had the idea of building an ice boat of his own to use on the Gulf of Finland in winter. He got hold of some sort of pamphlet about ice boats and procured some lumber, which he and Alik brought into the room—with the result that it immediately became impossible not only to sweep the floor but even to get from one part of the room to another. The dining table had to be shoved up against the wall, the couch against the window; it lay in a huge pile on the floor, and Olga Petrovna was constantly tripping over it. But all her entreaties were in vain. It was useless for her to explain to Kolya and Alik that she couldn't have been more uncomfortable if they had brought an elephant into the house. They went on planing, measuring, drawing plans and sawing until they became absolutely convinced that the author of the pamphlet on ice boats was an ignoramus, and that no ice boat could ever be constructed from his plans.

Whereupon they simply sawed up the lumber and meekly burned it in the stove, together with the pamphlet. Olga Petrovna put the furniture back in place, and for a whole week couldn't get over the pleasure of the space and cleanliness of her room.

At first the radio too caused Olga Petrovna nothing but

inconvenience. Kolya and Alik crammed the room full of wiring, screws, nuts and bolts, and bits of wood; they were up till two every morning discussing the relative merits of various types of receiver. Then they finally constructed the receiver, but never let Olga Petrovna listen to anything to the end as they wanted to get something else, Norway perhaps, or England. Then a passion for perfection overcame them, and they spent every evening taking the set apart and putting it together again. Finally, Olga Petrovna took things into her own hands, and then it turned out that the radio was in fact a very pleasant invention. She learned how to switch it on and off herself, forbade Kolya and Alik to touch it and, in the evenings, listened to broadcasts of operas or concerts from the philharmonic.

Natasha Frolenko also used to come and listen. She brought her embroidery, and sat at the table working. She was clever with her hands, she knitted beautifully, sewed, embroidered napkins and collars. The walls of her own room were already completely covered with things she had embroidered, and now she started to embroider a tablecloth for Olga Petrovna.

On her days off Olga Petrovna switched on the radio first thing in the morning: she liked to hear the confident, important voice announcing that Perfumery Store No. 4 had received a large consignment of perfume and Eau de Cologne, or that a new operetta was to have its *première* in a few days. She just couldn't restrain herself and wrote down every telephone number that was given. The only thing that didn't interest her in the least was the latest news on the international situation. Kolya explained carefully to her all about the German fascists and Mussolini and Chiang Kai-shek—she listened, but only out of politeness. When she sat down on the couch to read the pa-

31

per, she only looked at the local news items, satirical pieces or the "News from the Courts"; but when she came to the editorials or news dispatches, she invariably fell asleep, and the newspaper dropped onto her face. What she liked much better than newspapers were the translations of foreign novels which Natasha borrowed from the library, like *The Green Hat* or *Hearts of Three*.

The eighth of March—Women's Day—became a happy day in Olga Petrovna's life. In the morning the messenger woman from the publishing house brought her a basket of flowers. Among the flowers was a card inscribed:

"To Olga Petrovna Lipatova, non-Party worker, on the occasion of the eighth of March.
        From the Party Organization and the Mestkom"

She put the flowers on Kolya's desk under the shelf with Lenin's collected works and next to the miniature bust of Stalin. All day she felt happy. She decided not to throw the flowers away when they wilted, but to dry them and put them away in a book as a souvenir.

Olga Petrovna was in her third year at the office. Her pay had been raised and she no longer received two hundred and fifty rubles but three hundred and seventy-five. Kolya and Alik were still studying, but they were already earning quite a bit in some design office, drawing and doing industrial designs. For Olga Petrovna's birthday, Kolya bought her a little tea service, out of his own money: a teapot, milk jug, sugar bowl and three cups and saucers. The porcelain was thin, of good quality, only Olga Petrovna didn't really like the pattern on it very much—sort of squares, red on yellow. She would have preferred flowers. . . . But that didn't matter. It was a present from her son.

And her son had become handsome, gray eyes, black eyebrows, tall, full of calm self-confidence and gay. Fyodor

Ivanovich had never been quite like that, even in his best years. He was always smart-looking in a military way, clean and vigorous. Olga Petrovna would look at him with tenderness but with a constant undercurrent of anxiety; rejoicing, yet afraid to rejoice. A very good-looking youth, healthy too, he didn't drink and he didn't smoke, was a good son and a loyal Komsomol member. Of course Alik too was a polite young man, and hard-working, but nothing like Kolya! His father was a bookbinder in Vinnitsa in the Ukraine. He had masses of children and lived in poverty. Alik, ever since he was quite small, had lived with an aunt in Leningrad. But she evidently didn't look after him very well: the elbows of his jacket were all patched, his shoes were shabby. He was short and puny. And then he hadn't a brain as good as Kolya's.

There was one thing constantly worrying Olga Petrovna: Kolya was already over twenty, and he still had no room of his own. She kept on wondering whether her constant presence was not preventing Kolya from leading his own life. Kolya apparently had fallen in love with some girl at the institute. She questioned Alik about it, discreetly: who was she, what was her name, and how old was she? Was she a good student? Who were her parents? But Alik's answers were evasive, and the look in his eyes showed that he was not going to give the secret away. All Olga Petrovna managed to get out of him was the girl's name—Lilya. But it didn't matter what her name was, nor whether it was a really serious love or just infatuation—the fact remained that it was absolutely essential for a young man of his age to have a separate room.

Olga Petrovna confided her worries in Natasha. Natasha listened without saying a word, then blushed and said that yes . . . naturally . . . of course . . . Nikolai Fyodorovich would be better off in a room of his own . . . but, well . . . she for instance lived by herself with no mother . . . and yet—there was nothing!

Natasha broke off in confusion and fell silent, and Olga Petrovna never did understand what it was she actually wanted to say.

Olga Petrovna considered all possible ways whereby she could exchange her one room for two, and even began to put money into her savings bank so as to be able to pay more, if necessary.

But the question of a separate room for Kolya suddenly ceased to be urgent: the honor students at the institute, Nikolai Lipatov and Aleksandr Finkelstein, were to be sent as experts under some labor appointment scheme or other to Uralmash (Ural Engineering Works) in Sverdlovsk. They were short of engineering and technical workers there. The institute made arrangements for them to complete their studies by correspondence.

"Don't worry, Mama," Kolya said, putting his great big hand on Olga Petrovna's little one. "Don't worry, Alik and I will manage wonderfully there. . . . They have promised us a room in a dormitory . . . and Sverdlovsk is not very far away, after all. You'll be able to come and see us some time . . . and . . . you know what? You can send us parcels."

Every day after that, when she returned from the office, Olga Petrovna immediately began sorting out Kolya's clothes in the dresser, sewing, mending and ironing his things. She took Fyodor Ivanovich's old suitcase to be repaired. She remembered the spring morning when she and Fyodor Ivanovich bought that suitcase together at the Guard Regiment's store, but it now appeared to be infinitely remote—some kind of unreal morning from some kind of unreal life. She looked curiously at the page of the *Niva* which had been used to fix a tear in the side of the suitcase: the lady in the low-necked dress with the long train and her hair piled up on the top of her head struck her as strange. That's what the fashions were like in those days.

Kolya's departure worried Olga Petrovna and made her sad, but she couldn't help admiring the skill and care with which he packed his books and the large notebooks filled with his neat writing; and himself sewed his Komsomol membership card into the waist of his trousers.

For a long time the day of his departure was a week away—then suddenly it turned out to be tomorrow.

"Kolya, are you ready? Kolya!" asked Alik, coming into their room in the morning. His new jacket was rucked up on the shoulders, the corners of his shirt collar crumpled.

Kolya strode over to his suitcase and picked it up as easily as if it had been empty. All the way to the station he was practically waving the suitcase without even stopping for breath, but poor Alik shuffled along with his little chest, puffing and wiping the sweat off his brow with his jacket sleeve. With his short legs and his big head with the protruding ears, he reminded Olga Petrovna of some comic little figure out of a cartoon film. Alik's aunt, of course, couldn't be bothered to go to the station to see him off, so the three of them—Kolya, Olga Petrovna and Alik—walked solemnly up and down the platform in the damp gloom of the station.

Kolya and Alik were having a heated discussion on the question: which is more durable and lighter—the Fiat or the Packard? And it was not until five minutes before the train was to depart that Olga Petrovna remembered she had neither warned the boys to beware of thieves on the trip nor given them instructions about their laundry. They must never give things to the laundress without first counting them and making a list. . . . And never on any account eat vinaigrette salad in a canteen: it was often left over from the day before—and it was so easy to get typhoid fever. She took Alik aside and clutched his shoulders.

"Alik, my dear," she entreated, "please look after Kolya for me. . . ."

Alik looked at her through his glasses with his big, kind eyes.

"That's no trouble, is it? Of course I'll keep an eye on Nikolai. What else?"

It was time to get into the train. A moment later Kolya and Alik appeared at the window, Kolya tall, Alik up to his shoulder. Kolya said something to Olga Petrovna, but it couldn't be heard through the glass. He laughed, took off his cap and looked around the compartment, happy and excited. Alik was forming letters for Olga Petrovna with his fingers: "Don't" . . . she made out, and waved to him, guessing what he wanted to say: "Don't worry." . . . My God, they are mere children and they go off on such a journey!

A moment later she was walking back along the platform, alone in the crowd, walking faster and faster without noticing where she was going, wiping her eyes with the back of her hand.

## FIVE

After Kolya's departure, Olga Petrovna spent even less time at home. There was always enough overtime work at the office, and she stayed late nearly every evening, saving up money to buy Kolya a suit: a young engineer had to dress decently.

On her free evenings she took Natasha home with her for tea. They would stop together at the food store on the corner and choose two pastries. Olga Petrovna would make tea in the teapot with the squares on it, and turn on the radio. Natasha brought her embroidery. Recently, on Olga Petrovna's advice, she had been taking brewer's yeast regularly, but her complexion didn't get any better.

On one such evening, just as she was leaving Olga Petrovna's to go home, Natasha suddenly asked her to give her Kolya's latest photo.

"The only photo I've got in my room now is my mother's," she explained.

Olga Petrovna gave her the photo of Kolya, handsome and big-eyed, in a collar and tie. The photographer had caught his smile perfectly.

One day, on the way back from work, they went into a movie—and from then onward the movies became their favorite form of entertainment. They both loved films about airmen and border guards. Olga Petrovna thought the handsome, smiling airmen, who performed such great feats, looked like Kolya. She liked the new songs resounding from the screen—particularly "Thank You, My Heart," and "When My Country Calls on Me to Be a Hero." She liked the word "Homeland." This word, written with a capital letter, gave her a warm, proud feeling. And when the finest airman or the most courageous frontier guard fell, flat on his back, struck down by an enemy bullet, Olga Petrovna clutched Natasha's hand, just as, in her youth, she used to clutch Fyodor Ivanovich's hand, when Vera Kholodnaya would suddenly produce a miniature revolver from her wide muff and raise it slowly and aim at the vile villain's forehead.

Natasha again applied for admission to the Komsomol, and was again refused. Olga Petrovna deeply sympathized with Natasha's grief; the poor girl was so much in need of company. . . . And anyway, why, in fact, should she not be admitted? The girl was a hard worker and absolutely loyal to the Soviet regime. For one thing, she worked excellently, better than any of them. And then, she was politically aware. Not like Olga Petrovna. She never let a day pass without reading *Pravda* from beginning to end. Natasha was up on everything, no less than Kolya and Alik—the international situation as well as construction under the five-year plan, everything.

And how she worried when the *Chelushkin* was crushed by the ice! She remained glued to the radio. She cut out of the newspapers all the photographs of Captain Voronin, of Schmidt's camp and then of the pilots. When the news of the first rescues were announced, she wept over her typewriter, tears falling onto the paper, and was so overjoyed that she messed up two pages. "They won't let people perish, they won't," she repeated, wiping her eyes. Such a sincere, warmhearted girl. And now the Komsomol had turned her down again. It was unjust.

Olga Petrovna even wrote to Kolya about the injustice that befell Natasha. But Kolya replied that injustice was a class concept, and vigilance was essential. Natasha did after all come from a bourgeois, landowning family. Vile fascist hirelings, of the kind that had murdered comrade Kirov, had still not been eradicated in the entire country. Class struggle was continuing and, therefore, it was essential to exercise the utmost vigilance when admitting people to the Party and the Komsomol. He also wrote that in a few years Natasha would, no doubt, be admitted, and strongly advised her to take notes on the works of Lenin, Stalin, Marx and Engels.

"In a few years . . ." Natasha smiled bitterly. "Nikolai Fyodorovich forgets that I shall soon be twenty-four."

"Then you'll be admitted straight into the Party," Olga Petrovna told her consolingly. "And what's twenty-four! It is only the first youth."

Natasha didn't answer but, when leaving for home that evening, she asked Olga Petrovna for a volume of Kolya's Lenin.

Kolya's letters arrived regularly every week, on Saturdays. What a wonderful son he was—never forgot that his mother worried about him, though he had plenty to do there! When she returned from work, Olga Petrovna would

41

start getting her key out of her bag while she was still at the bottom of the stairs, rush up and, when she finally reached the fourth floor, out of breath, she would open the blue mailbox. The yellow envelope was already there awaiting her. Sitting down by the window, still in her coat, she would spread out the carefully folded sheets of Kolya's letter, written on notebook paper.

"Hello, Mama!" every letter began. "I hope you are well. I'm fine. Production at our plant in the past week was . . ."

The letters were long, but mostly about the plant, the growth of the Stakhanovite movement; about himself and his life—not a word.

"Just think," Kolya wrote in his first letter, "all the worm gears, milling cutters, even the broaches, everything we have is still foreign-made. We pay gold to the capitalists for everything—we ourselves are still unable to produce them."

But Olga Petrovna was not interested in milling cutters. What she wanted to know was what he and Alik were getting to eat, whether the laundress there was honest; had they enough money? And when did they have time to study? At night, or when? But Kolya merely skimmed over all these questions, or wrote something incomprehensible. Olga Petrovna so longed to be able to imagine what their room was like, how they lived and what they ate that, on Natasha's advice, she decided to write to Alik.

The answer came a few days later.

"Dear Olga Petrovna!" Alik wrote. "Forgive me for putting it so bluntly, but you're quite wrong to worry about Nikolai's health. We eat quite well. I buy sausage in the evenings and fry it in butter for breakfast. We have lunch in the canteen, three courses, not bad at all. The preserves you sent we decided to have only with our evening tea, this way it will last us a long time. I also look after the laundry, and count it. We have allotted a certain time every day for study. You may be absolutely assured that I do everything I can for Nikolai, as his friend and comrade."

And the letter ended:

"Nikolai is successfully developing a method for the production of Fellows' cogwheel cutters in our machine-tool workshop. The people on the plant Party committee say he's the rising eagle of the future."

Of course it is the sun that rises, and not eagles, and Olga Petrovna had no idea what a Fellows' cogwheel cutter was—but still, these words filled her heart with pride and admiration.

Olga Petrovna put Kolya's letters carefully away into a box which had once contained writing paper. There too she kept the letters Fyodor Ivanovich had written her when they were engaged, the photographs of Kolya when he was little, and the photograph of the infant Karina, born aboard the *Chelushkin*. Olga Petrovna also put Alik's letter there. She was fond of Alik: he was undoubtedly devoted to Kolya, and understood him very well.

One day, about ten months after Kolya's departure, Olga Petrovna received through the mail an impressive-looking plywood crate. Sent from Sverdlovsk. From Kolya. The crate was so heavy that the mailman had a hard time bringing it into the room, and demanded a ruble as a tip. "A sewing machine, perhaps?" thought Olga Petrovna. "That would be great!" She had sold hers when times were hard.

The mailman left. Olga Petrovna took a hammer and knife and opened the box. Inside lay a mysterious black steel object. It was carefully packed in wood shavings. Not exactly a wheel, not a bore either. God knows what. Then at last, on the black back of the mysterious object, Olga Petrovna discovered a label, on which was written, in Kolya's writing: "Dear Mother, I'm sending you the first cogwheel cut with the Fellows' cogwheel cutter produced in our plant by my method."

Olga Petrovna laughed, patted the cogwheel and, puffing, hoisted it onto the window sill. Every time she looked at it, she felt cheerful.

A few days after that, when Olga Petrovna was finishing her morning tea, in a hurry to get to work, Natasha suddenly burst into her room. Her hair was disheveled and wet with snow, and one of her boots unfastened. She handed Olga Petrovna a wet newspaper.

"Look at this. . . . I've just bought it on the corner . . . I was just reading it . . . and suddenly I see: Nikolai Fyodorovich, Kolya."

There on the front page of *Pravda*, Olga Petrovna saw Kolya's smiling face. The photograph made him look different, a little older, but there could be no doubt about it, it was Kolya, her son.

Under the portrait was a caption:

Industrial enthusiast, Komsomol member NIKOLAI LI-PATOV, who has developed a method for the manufacture of Fellows' cogwheel cutters at the Ural Machine-building Plant.

Natasha embraced Olga Petrovna, and kissed her on the cheek.

"Dear Olga Petrovna," she entreated, "please, let's send him a telegram."

Olga Petrovna had never seen Natasha so excited. Her own hands were shaking, too, and she couldn't find her brief case. They composed the telegram at work during the lunch hour, and sent it off after work.

Everyone congratulated Olga Petrovna: at the office even Zoya Viktorovna congratulated her on having a son like that; at home even the accountant's wife.

As she went to bed that evening, happy and tired, it occurred to Olga Petrovna for the first time that Natasha was probably in love with Kolya. How could she not have guessed earlier! A good girl, well brought up, and hard-working—but so very plain, and older than him, too.

Half asleep, Olga Petrovna tried to picture to herself the girl whom Kolya would love and make his wife: tall, fresh, with pink cheeks and bright eyes and light hair—very much like an English post card, only with a KIM * badge pinned on her breast. Lilya? No, Svetlana would be better. Or Ludmila: Milochka.

* Communist Youth International—Translator.

45

## SIX

I t would soon be the New Year, the year 1937. The
Mestkom committee decided to have a party for the
children of the people working at the publishing house.
Olga Petrovna was put in charge of organizing it. She
picked Natasha as her assistant, and soon their work was
in full swing.

They telephoned the homes of the employees to find out
the names and ages of the children; typed out the invita-
tions; ran around the shops buying candy and honeycakes,
glass balls and party favors, and wore themselves out
looking for artificial snow.

The most important and most difficult thing was to
choose presents for the children and find something each
one would like without exceeding the sum available. Olga
Petrovna and Natasha almost came to quarreling about the

present for the director's little girl. Olga Petrovna wanted to buy her a big doll—bigger than for the other little girls—but Natasha thought that would be indelicate. They compromised on a pretty little trumpet with a fluffy tassel.

Finally, there remained only the New Year's tree to be bought. They bought a tall one, going right up to the ceiling, with thick, full branches. On the day of the party Natasha, Olga Petrovna and Marya Karpovna, the elevator woman, decorated it. It took them from early in the morning till two in the afternoon. Marya Karpovna entertained them with stories about the director's wife; to the director himself she referred, as people used to under the old regime, as "they." She handed Natasha and Olga Petrovna the glass globes and paper favors, the little mailboxes and silver ships, and Natasha and Olga Petrovna hung them on the tree.

Before long Olga Petrovna's feet began to ache, so she sat down and started placing little slips of paper with "Thank you, Comrade Stalin, for a happy childhood" written on them into the candy packets.

Natasha continued decorating the tree by herself. She had magic fingers and wonderfully good taste: the way she put up Grandfather Frost was really extremely effective. Then Olga Petrovna glued the curly head of the child Lenin in the center of a large, red, five-pointed star. Natasha put it up on the very top of the tree—and everything was ready. They removed the full-length portrait of Stalin from the wall and replaced it with another—of Stalin sitting with a little girl on his knee. That was the portrait Olga Petrovna liked best of all.

Three o'clock. Time to go home, rest a little, have dinner and then dress up for the party.

The party was a wonderful success. All the kids showed up and all the papas and mamas. The director's wife wasn't there, but the director came and brought his little daughter himself, an enchanting little girl with blond hair.

The children were delighted with their presents, the parents went into raptures over the tree. Only Anna Grigorievna, the chairman of the Mestkom committee, was offended because her son was given a drum and not wooden soldiers like those the son of the Party organizer received: the soldiers were more expensive. She was wearing a green dress, low-necked, even. Her son, a lanky, unpleasant little boy, whistled and ostentatiously broke the drum by banging his fist through it. But all the others were pleased. The director's little girl blew on her trumpet all the time, hopping up and down between her father's knees, pushing her chubby little hand against his leg and tipping her head backward to look at the tree.

Olga Petrovna felt like the real mistress of the ball. She wound up the Gramophone, switched on the radio, indicated to the elevator woman with her eyes to whom to offer the plates of candies. She felt sorry for Natasha: the girl was standing timidly against the wall, pale and gray looking, in her best blouse which she had embroidered herself. The director, bending down, took his little girl by both hands, led her up to the tree, and warned her that Grandfather Frost would be angry if she didn't behave. Olga Petrovna was touched as she watched this scene: she hoped Kolya would be just like the director. Who knows, in two years, perhaps, she too might have a sweet little girl like that as her granddaughter. Or a grandson. She would persuade Kolya to call her grandson Vladlen *—a lovely

* Vladimir Lenin—Translator.

49

name! Or if it was a granddaughter, Ninel—an elegant French-sounding name, and if you read it backward it became Lenin.

Olga Petrovna, tired out, sank down into a chair. She was thinking it was time she went home, she was beginning to get a migraine headache, when the impressive-looking accountant approached and, bowing politely, told her a fearful piece of news: a large number of physicians in the city had been arrested. The accountant was personally acquainted with all the leading medical men in town. His eczema resisted everyone's treatments, the late Fyodor Ivanovich was the only one who had succeeded in getting rid of it. ("There was a real doctor for you! The others sprinkle powders about, smear on ointments, but all to no effect. . . .")

Among those arrested, the accountant named Dr. Kiparisov, a colleague of Fyodor Ivanovich's and Kolya's godfather.

"What? Doctor Kiparisov? . . . It couldn't be! But what's happened? Surely not another . . . accident?" asked Olga Petrovna, not daring to pronounce the word "assassination."

The accountant raised his eyes helplessly and went away, walking on tiptoe for some reason.

Two years before, after the murder of Kirov—(Oh! What grim times those were! Patrols in the streets . . . and when Comrade Stalin was about to arrive the station square was cordoned off by troops . . . and there were troops lining all the streets as Stalin walked behind the coffin. . . .)—after that murder, there had also been many arrests, but at that time they first took all kinds of oppositionists, then old-regime people, all kinds of "vons" and barons. But now—it was doctors.

50

After the murder of Kirov, Madame Nezhentseva was sent away, as a member of the nobility. An old friend of Olga Petrovna's; they had even been at school together. At first Olga Petrovna had been astonished; what connection could Madame Nezhentseva have with the murder? She taught French in a school, and lived just like everyone else. But Kolya explained that it was essential to rid Leningrad of unreliable elements. "What exactly is this Madame Nezhentseva of yours, anyway? You remember yourself, Mama, that she didn't recognize Mayakovsky as a poet and always used to say that everything was cheaper in the old days. She is not a real Soviet person. . . ." All right, but what about the doctors? What were they guilty of? Just imagine—Boris Ignatyich Kiparisov! Such an esteemed doctor!

The children were noisy in the cloakroom. Olga Petrovna, acting as hostess, helped the parents to find boots and leggings. The director, carrying his daughter, came up to say good-by to her. He thanked the Mestkom for the splendid party.

"I saw the portrait of your son in *Pravda*," he told her with a smile. "It's a fine new generation growing up to take our place. . . ."

Olga Petrovna looked at him with adoration. She wanted to say that he had no right yet to talk about being replaced—what was thirty-five, after all? The prime of life! —but she didn't dare.

He dressed his little girl himself, wrapping her up in a fluffy white scarf over her little fur coat. How skillfully he did everything! Her mother didn't need to worry about letting him take the child out. A wonderful family man— one could see that at a glance.

## SEVEN

The papers said nothing about the doctors or about Dr. Kiparisov. Olga Petrovna intended to call on Mrs. Kiparisova, but couldn't bring herself to. There was no time, and anyway it was a bit awkward. She hadn't seen Mrs. Kiparisova for about three years. She couldn't very well suddenly go and visit her, out of the blue.

In January, articles began to appear in the papers about an upcoming new trial. The other trial, of Kamenev and Zinoviev, had made a great impression on Olga Petrovna, but she was too unused to reading the papers to follow it in detail every day. But this time Natasha got her into reading the papers, and they read all the articles about the trial together every day. There was more and more talk everywhere about fascist spies, and terrorists, and arrests. . . .

Just think, these scoundrels wanted to murder our beloved Stalin. It was they, it turned out, who had murdered

Kirov. They caused explosions in the mines and derailed trains. And there was scarcely an establishment in which they hadn't placed their henchmen.

One of the typists in the office, just back from a vacation resort, related that there was a young engineer who lived in the room next to theirs, she sometimes even went for walks with him in the park. Then one night a car suddenly drove up, and he was arrested: it turned out he was a saboteur. Yet he looked like such a decent person—you never could tell.

In Olga Petrovna's house too, in apartment 104 opposite hers, someone was arrested—some Communist or other. His room was closed up with red seals on the door. The house manager told Olga Petrovna about it.

In the evenings, Olga Petrovna put on her glasses—she had recently become farsighted—and read the paper aloud to Natasha. The tablecloth was already finished, and Natasha was now embroidering a cover for Olga Petrovna's bed.

They discussed how indignant Kolya must be just now. And not Kolya alone either: all decent people were indignant. Why, the trains derailed by the saboteurs might contain children! What utter heartlessness! Monsters! It was not for nothing that the Trotskyites were hand in glove with the Gestapo: they were really no better than the fascists, who were murdering children in Spain. And was it really possible that Dr. Kiparisov had taken part in the activities of this bandit gang? He had quite often been summoned for consultation together with Fyodor Ivanovich. Afterward Fyodor Ivanovich would bring him home to have a cup of tea. Olga Petrovna had seen him close up, just as close as Natasha was to her now. And now he had joined that bandit gang? Who could have thought it? Such a worthy old man.

One evening, after reading in the paper about all the crimes committed by the accused and hearing the same thing repeated on the radio, she and Natasha had such a vivid picture of heaps of mutilated bodies with the arms and legs torn off that Olga Petrovna was afraid to remain by herself in the room, and Natasha was afraid to walk home through the streets. That night Natasha stayed with her, and slept on her couch.

Everywhere, in every enterprise and every establishment, meetings were held, and the publishing house held one too, to discuss the trial. The chairman of the Mestkom went around to all the rooms beforehand, warning all that in case anyone had so little sense of responsibility as to intend leaving before the meeting, he would do well to bear in mind that the outside door would be locked. Absolutely everyone came to the meeting, even the members of the editorial section, who usually skipped them.

The director made a speech containing a brief, dry and precise summary of the information given in the papers. He was followed by the Party organizer, Comrade Timofeyev. Pausing after every few words, he declared that the enemies of the people were active everywhere, that they might infiltrate even into this establishment and that it was therefore essential for all honest workers to increase incessantly their political vigilance. The chairman of the Mestkom, Anna Grigorievna, was then given the floor.

"Comrades!" she began, then closed her eyes and was silent for a moment. "Comrades!" She clasped her thin hands with the long nails. "The vile enemy has thrust out his dirty paw into our establishment too!"

There was a gasp of horror. The cameo on Anna Grigorievna's ample bosom rose and fell.

"Arrested last night was the ex-supervisor of our print shop, now unmasked as an enemy of the people—Kuzmin. He turned out to be a nephew of the Moscow Kuzmin who was unmasked a month ago. With the connivance of our Party organization which is suffering, to use Comrade Stalin's apt expression, from the idiotic disease of complacency, Kuzmin continued, so to speak, to 'operate' in our print shop even after his own uncle, the Moscow Kuzmin, had been unmasked."

She sat down, her breast heaving.

"No questions?" asked the director, who was presiding at this meeting.

"But what did they . . . do . . . in the print shop?" Natasha asked timidly.

The director nodded at the chairman of the Mestkom.

"What did they do?" she repeated in a shrill voice, rising from her chair. "I think, Comrade Frolenko, I explained clearly enough, right here, that the ex-supervisor of our print shop, Kuzmin, turned out to be the nephew of the other Kuzmin, the Moscow one. He maintained daily contact with his uncle . . . undermined the Stakhanovite movement in the print shop . . . wrecked the plan . . . on the orders of his relative. With the criminal connivance of our Party organization."

Natasha asked nothing more.

Returning home after the meeting, Olga Petrovna sat down to write a letter to Kolya. She told him that enemies had been discovered in their print shop. How were things at the Uralmash Plant? Was everything going well there? It was up to Kolya, as a loyal Komsomol member, to be on his guard.

At the publishing house, there was a distinct feeling of uneasiness. The director was summoned daily to the Smolny.* The sullen Party organizer was constantly coming into the typing office, unlocking the door with his own private latchkey—and calling Zoya Viktorovna into the special department. The nice polite accountant, who somehow always knew everything that was going on, told Olga Petrovna that the Party organization was now meeting every evening.

"There's a bit of a stink," he said with a knowing smile. "Anna Grigorievna is blaming everything on the Party organizer, and the Party organizer is blaming the director. From what I understand, there's going to be a change of management."

"Blamed for what?" asked Olga Petrovna.

"Well, they simply can't agree which of them it was that let Kuzmin slip through."

Olga Petrovna didn't get it clearly at all, and left the office that day with a vague feeling of alarm.

On the street, she noticed a tall old woman wearing a scarf over her hat, in felt boots with galoshes over them, and with a cane. The old woman walked, seeking out spots that were not slippery with her stick. Her face seemed familiar to Olga Petrovna. Why, it was Mrs. Kiparisova! Could it really be she? Good God, how she had changed!

"Nina Vassilyevna!" Olga Petrovna called out to her.

Mrs. Kiparisova stopped, raised her large black eyes and, with an obvious effort, managed a pleasant smile.

"How are you, Olga Petrovna! It's ages since we met! Your son must be quite grown up." She stood there clasping Olga Petrovna's hand, not looking her in the face. Her great big eyes darted all around in confusion.

* Leningrad Party Headquarters—Translator.

"Nina Vassilyevna," said Olga Petrovna warmly, "I'm so glad I ran into you. I heard that there's been unpleasantness . . . with Boris Ignatyich. . . . Listen, we're friends after all. . . . Boris Ignatyich was Kolya's godfather . . . that doesn't count any more of course, but we belong to the old times, you and I. Tell me, is Boris Ignatyich being accused of anything serious? Surely there can't be any kind of grounds for these accusations? I simply can't believe it, I can't. Such a fine, such an honorable doctor! My husband always had the greatest respect for him, and looked up to him as a clinical physician."

"Boris Ignatyich did nothing against the Soviet regime,'" said Mrs. Kiparisova gloomily.

"I thought not!" exclaimed Olga Petrovna. "I didn't doubt it for a moment, and said so to everyone . . ."

Kiparisova looked at her somberly with her great dark eyes.

"Good-by, Olga Petrovna," she said, without a smile.

"When Boris Ignatyich returns, you must invite me over," Olga Petrovna went on. "Why are you so upset about it? Since Boris Ignatyich is not guilty, why, everything will be all right. In our country nothing can happen to an honest person. It's simply a misunderstanding. Don't be downhearted, my dear. . . . Come and have a cup of tea someday."

She watched Nina Kiparisova start walking along the pavement, tapping the ice with her stick.

"Could I have aged that much too?" thought Olga Petrovna. "Her face is all dark and wrinkled. No, it's impossible, I don't look like that yet. She just let herself go! Felt boots, stick and a scarf . . . It's very important for a woman not to let herself go, to take care of herself. Who on earth wears felt boots these days? It's not nineteen-

58

eighteen! Why, she looked like sixty-five, though she can't be more than fifty. . . . It's a good thing that Kiparisov isn't guilty. A wife should know, if anyone can. I always thought it was simply a misunderstanding, and nothing else."

## EIGHT

The next day the typing pool was rushing to finish the semiannual report, which had to be completed urgently. Everyone knew that the director was leaving that night by the *Red Arrow* for Moscow, to report the following day to the Press Department of the Party Central Committee on the half-year's work of the publishing house. Olga Petrovna urged the typists to hurry. Natasha worked straight through the lunch hour without a break.

By three o'clock, the report was already on Olga Petrovna's desk, and she carefully sorted out the four copies, clipping the pages together evenly.

Still the director's secretary didn't come to pick up the report. Olga Petrovna decided to take it to the director's office herself.

The door was half open; she bumped into the Party organizer on the threshold.

"You can't go in there!" he said, without even nodding a greeting to her, and limped away into another room. He looked all disheveled.

Olga Petrovna glanced through the half-open door. Kneeling in front of the desk was a stranger, pulling papers out of a drawer. There were papers strewn all over the carpet.

"What time will Comrade Zakharov be here today?" Olga Petrovna asked the elderly secretary.

"He's been arrested," the secretary answered by moving her lips silently, "last night."

Her lips were blue.

Olga Petrovna took the report back to her office. As she reached the office door, she felt her knees giving way under her.

The clatter of the typewriters deafened her. "Do they know already or not?" They clattered on, as though nothing had happened. If she had been told the director had died she wouldn't have been quite so stunned. She sat down at her desk and began mechanically taking the clips off the sheets of paper.

Timofeyev came in, opening the door with his own key as usual. Olga Petrovna noticed for the first time that, despite his lameness, the Party organizer held himself erect and walked with a firm step. "Excuse me!" she said, in a frightened voice, when he brushed her with his shoulder accidentally in passing.

At four-thirty the bell rang at last. Olga Petrovna went silently downstairs, silently put on her coat and hat and went out into the street. It was thawing. Olga Petrovna stopped in front of a puddle, pondering how to get around it, when Natasha came up to her. Natasha knew already. Zoya Viktorovna had told her.

"Natasha," Olga Petrovna began, when they came to the corner where they usually parted, "Natasha, do you really believe that Zakharov is guilty of anything? It's nonsense. . . . Natasha, we do know . . ."

She was simply at a loss for words to express her confidence in him. Zakharov, a Bolshevik, their director whom they'd seen every day, Zakharov a saboteur! It was an impossibility, fantastic nonsense, balderdash, as Fyodor Ivanovich used to say. A misunderstanding? But he was such an eminent Party man! They knew him both at the Smolny and in Moscow, he couldn't have been arrested by mistake. He wasn't just anyone, like Kiparisov!

Natasha said nothing.

"Let's stop at your place, I'll explain everything," Natasha said suddenly, with unusual solemnity.

They went in and took off their coats in silence. Natasha took a carefully folded newspaper out of her shabby brief case. She opened the paper and pointed out a special article on the middle page to Olga Petrovna.

Olga Petrovna put on her glasses.

"You understand, my dear, he could have been enticed," whispered Natasha, "a woman . . ."

Olga Petrovna began to read.

The article recounted the case of a certain Soviet citizen, A., a loyal Party member, who was sent by the Soviet Government on a mission to Germany to study the use of a new chemical. In Germany, he fulfilled his duties conscientiously, but soon he became involved with a certain S., an elegant young woman who professed to be sympathetic to the Soviet Union. S. paid frequent visits to citizen A. in his apartment. Then one day A. discovered that certain important political documents were missing from his office. The landlady informed him that S. had come to his room when he was not there. A. had sufficient courage to break off with S. immediately, but not sufficient courage to tell his comrades about the disappearance of the documents. He went back to the Soviet Union hoping, by his honest work as a Soviet engineer, to atone for the crime against his homeland. For a whole year he worked peacefully, and was beginning to forget about his crime. But the hidden agents of the Gestapo, infiltrating into our country, began to blackmail him. Terrorized by them, A. handed over the secret plans of the plant where he was working. The valiant Chekists * unmasked the entrenched agents of fascism: the investigation led back to the unfortunate A.

"You understand?" asked Natasha in a whisper. "The investigation . . . Our director is of course a fine person, a loyal Party member. But citizen A. too, they write here, was a loyal Party member at first. . . . Any loyal Party member can be led astray by a pretty face."

Natasha could not stand pretty women. She recognized only classical beauty, but couldn't find it in anyone.

"They say that our director has been abroad," Natasha remarked. "Also on a mission. You remember the elevator woman, Marya Karpovna saying that he brought his wife a light-blue knitted suit from Berlin?"

The article upset Olga Petrovna a great deal, but she still couldn't believe it. This Comrade A. was one thing, but their own Zakharov was quite another. A staunch Party member; he had himself reported about the investigation. And under him, the publishing house had always over-fulfilled its plan.

"But, Natasha, we do know . . ." said Olga Petrovna wearily.

"What do we know?" retorted Natasha hotly. "We

* Members of the Secret Police—Translator.

64

know that he was the director of our publishing house, and actually we don't know any more than that. Do you know everything about his life? Can you really vouch for him?"

And indeed, Olga Petrovna had not the slightest idea how Comrade Zakharov spent his time when he was not presiding at the meetings of the publishing house personnel or leading his little girl up to the New Year's tree. Men, all men without exception, were terribly fond of pretty faces. Any cheeky housemaid could twist any man, even a decent one, around her little finger. If Olga Petrovna hadn't thrown Fanny out in time, there is no telling how her flirting with Fyodor Ivanovich might have ended.

"Let's have some tea," suggested Olga Petrovna.

Over tea, they remembered that there was something military about Zakharov's bearing. Straight back and broad shoulders. Perhaps he'd been a White officer in his time? He was old enough to have been.

They had nothing to eat with their tea. They were both too tired to be bothered going down to the shop to buy any buns or pastry. "It's going to be grim at the office tomorrow," thought Olga Petrovna. "Like having a corpse in the house. Say what you like, but one's sorry for the director." She remembered the half-open door of his office and the man on his knees in front of the desk. Only now she realized that it was an NKVD agent. It was a search.

Natasha got ready to leave. She carefully folded the paper and put it in her brief case. Then she poured some hot water into her glass and warmed her large red hands on it before going out. Her hands had been frostbitten as a child, and they were always chilly.

Suddenly there was a ring at the door, and then a second ring. Olga Petrovna went to open it. Two rings—that was for her. Who could have come this late?

Behind the door stood Alik Finkelstein.

To see Alik there alone, without Kolya—it was unnatural . . .

"Kolya?" exclaimed Olga Petrovna, grabbing Alik by the dangling end of his scarf. "Typhoid?"

Alik, without looking at her, slowly took off his galoshes.

"Shhh!" he said at last. "Let's go into your room."

And he tiptoed along the corridor, spreading his short legs wide apart.

Olga Petrovna, beside herself with anxiety, followed him.

"Only don't get frightened, for God's sake, Olga Petrovna," he said, when she had closed the door. "Calm down, please, Olga Petrovna. There's nothing to be frightened about. It's nothing terrible. The day before the day before yesterday . . . or when was it? Anyway, the day before the last day off, anyway . . . Kolya was arrested."

He sat down on the sofa, tore off his scarf with two jerks, threw it down on the floor and started weeping.

## NINE

She must rush off somewhere at once and clear up this monstrous misunderstanding. She must go immediately to Sverdlovsk and get hold of lawyers, prosecutors, judges, investigators. Olga Petrovna put on her coat, hat and boots, and took the money out of a box. She mustn't forget her passport . . . off to the station at once to buy a ticket!

But Alik, wiping his face with his scarf, said that, in his opinion, going to Sverdlovsk at once would be absolutely pointless. Kolya, as a native of Leningrad who had only recently gone to Sverdlovsk, would most probably be brought to Leningrad. Wouldn't she do better to put off the trip to Sverdlovsk for a while? Suppose she and Kolya missed each other?

Olga Petrovna took off her coat, and threw her papers and money on the table.

"The keys! Did you leave the keys there?" she cried suddenly, stepping up to Alik. "Did you leave the keys with someone?"

"Keys? What keys?" Alik was dumfounded.

"Oh, Lord! how stupid you are!" Olga Petrovna blurted out, then suddenly broke into sobs.

Natasha ran up to her and put her arms around her shoulders.

"But the keys . . . of the room . . . in your, what-do-you-call-it . . . your hostel?"

They still didn't understand, and looked at her in bewilderment. What fools they were! Olga Petrovna had a lump in her throat, and couldn't speak. Natasha poured a glass of water and handed it to her.

"But he . . . but he's . . ." sobbed Olga Petrovna, pushing the glass aside, "but he's . . . they must already have let him out . . . seen it's the wrong person . . . let him out . . . he's returned home and found you gone . . . and the key gone . . . there'll soon be a telegram from him."

Still in her boots, Olga Petrovna sank down onto her bed. She wept with her head buried in the pillow; she wept for a long time until her cheek and the pillow were wet. When she sat up, her face hurt and she could feel her heart thumping in her breast.

Natasha and Alik were whispering by the window.

"Here's what," said Alik, his kind eyes looking at her pityingly from under his glasses, "Natalya Sergeyevna and I have decided to do. You just go to bed now—and in the morning go quietly to the prosecutor's office. Natalya Sergeyevna will tell them at the office in the morning that you're ill . . . or something else . . . that you got poisoned by fumes in the night . . . I don't know what."

Alik went. Natasha wanted to stay for the night there but Olga Petrovna said she needed nothing, nothing. So Natasha kissed her and went. She looked as if she'd been weeping too.

Olga Petrovna washed her face in cold water, undressed, and lay down. In the darkness, the room was lit up at times by the lightninglike flashes from the streetcar wires. On the wall and ceiling was a square white patch of light, like a piece of folded paper. In the accountant's room the nurse was still scolding while Valya was laughing and squealing.

Olga Petrovna visualized Kolya being taken, under escort, to the official investigator. The investigator—a handsome military man, with straps and pockets everywhere.

"Nikolai Fomich Lipatov?" he asked Kolya.

"My name is Nikolai Fyodorovich Lipatov," replies Kolya, with dignity.

Whereupon the investigator sternly reprimands the escort and presents his apologies to Kolya.

"Well!" he exclaims. "How didn't I recognize you at once? Why you are—that young engineer whose picture I recently saw in *Pravda!* Please forgive me. The point is that a namesake of yours, Nikolai Fomich Lipatov, is a Trotskyite, a fascist hireling and a saboteur."

Olga Petrovna lay awake all night waiting for a telegram. Upon returning home to the hostel and finding out that Alik had left for Leningrad, Kolya would immediately send a telegram to reassure his mother. About six in the morning when the streetcars had again started screeching, Olga Petrovna fell asleep. She was awakened by a shrill ring which seemed to go straight to her heart. A telegram? But there was no second ring.

Olga Petrovna got dressed, washed, and forced herself to drink some tea and tidy up the room a little. Then she went

69

out into the street in the half light. It was still thawing, but a thin sheet of ice had formed on the puddles during the night.

After taking a few steps, Olga Petrovna stopped short. Where, actually, should she go?

Alik had said to the prosecutor's office. But Olga Petrovna didn't know precisely what the prosecutor's office was, or where it was. The thought of asking passers-by about a place like that filled her with shame. So she went not to the prosecutor's office but to the prison, since she happened to know that the prison was on Shpalernaya Street.

Outside the iron gates there was a sentry with a rifle. The small side door next to the main gate was locked. Olga Petrovna kept trying the door first with her hand, then with her knee, but in vain. There was no sign of any notice anywhere.

The sentry came up to her. "They'll start letting people in at nine," he announced. "The gate will be opened at nine."

It was twenty to eight. Olga Petrovna decided not to go home. She walked back and forth outside the prison, craning her head upward and gazing at the iron gratings.

Could it really be that Kolya was there, in that building, behind those iron gratings?

"You are not allowed to walk here, citizeness," the sentry warned her sternly.

Olga Petrovna crossed over to the other side of the street and walked on mechanically. On her left she saw the wide, snowy expanse of the Neva.

She turned down a street on the left and came out onto the embankment.

Day came. It became light. On the Liteynyy Bridge, all the lamps went out in amazing unison, as though on command. The Neva was piled up with heaps of dirty, yellowish snow. "I suppose the snow from all over the city is dumped here," thought Olga Petrovna.

She noticed a large crowd of women in the middle of the street. Some were leaning against the parapet of the embankment, others walking slowly back and forth along the sidewalk or on the pavement.

Olga Petrovna was surprised to see that they were all very warmly dressed, muffled in scarves on top of their coats, and nearly all of them in felt boots and galoshes. They were stamping their feet and blowing on their hands. "Obviously they must have been standing here a long time to have gotten so cold," reflected Olga Petrovna. "It's not freezing, but thawing again." All these women looked as if they'd been waiting for a train for hours at some wayside station.

Olga Petrovna took a careful look at the house opposite which the women were crowding—an ordinary house, without any signs on it. What were they waiting for? In the crowd there were both ladies in elegant coats and simple women. For lack of anything better to do, Olga Petrovna wandered once or twice through the crowd. One woman was holding a baby in her arms and another child, muffled crosswise in a scarf, by the hand. Near the wall of the house there was a man standing alone. All their faces were a greenish color—or perhaps it was only the morning half light that made them look like that.

A neatly dressed little old woman with a cane suddenly came up to Olga Petrovna. Under her sealskin cap, pulled down low on her forehead, showed strands of silver hair and dark, Semitic eyes.

"You want the list?" she asked in a friendly way. "In the front hall of Number Twenty-eight."

"What list?"

"For L and M . . . Oh, I'm sorry, citizeness! You are walking up and down here, so I thought you'd also come about someone who'd been arrested."

"Yes, about my son . . ." said Olga Petrovna in bewilderment.

Turning away from the old woman, upset by her surprising perspicacity, Olga Petrovna went to look for the main entrance of house Number Twenty-eight. The thought that all these women had come here for the same reason as she had filled her with vague foreboding. But why were they here, on the embankment, and not outside the prison? Oh, yes, the sentry doesn't allow waiting outside the prison.

Number Twenty-eight turned out to be a private residence with the paint peeling off, almost at the bridge. Olga Petrovna went into the main vestibule—luxurious but dirty, with a fireplace, a huge broken mirror and a marble cupid with one wing missing. On the first step of the majestic staircase lay a woman, curled up on a newspaper, her head propped up on a shabby old brief case.

"You want your name on the list?" she asked, raising her head. Then she sat up and pulled a pencil and a crumpled sheet of paper out of her brief case.

"I . . . really don't know," said Olga Petrovna distractedly. "I've come to see someone about my son, who was arrested by mistake in Sverdlovsk. . . . You understand, they simply mistook him for someone else of the same name."

"Speak lower, please," the woman irritatedly interrupted her. She had an educated, tired face. "Lists are taken away, and anyway . . . What's the name?"

"Lipatov," Olga Petrovna replied timidly.

"Three forty-four," the woman said, writing it down. "Your number is three forty-four. Go away from here please."

"Three forty-four," repeated Olga Petrovna, and went out onto the embankment again.

The crowd was still growing.

"What's your number?" people kept asking Olga Petrovna.

Automatically, she kept on repeating it.

"You won't get in today then," said a woman muffled up in a scarf, peasant-fashion. "We put our names on the list yesterday evening."

"Where's the list?" others were asking in a whisper.

It was quite light now.

Then suddenly all the people in the crowd began to run. Olga Petrovna ran behind them. A child bundled up in a scarf began to cry loudly. He had bandy little legs and barely managed to keep up with his mother.

The crowd turned down Shpalernaya Street. Olga Petrovna saw from a distance that the small door next to the iron gates was already open. People were squeezing into it like into a streetcar door. Olga Petrovna shoved through too, then stopped. There was nowhere else to go.

People were crowding in the semidark anteroom around a little wooden staircase. The crowd swayed back and forth. People were untying their scarves, unbuttoning their collars and elbowing their way about, each looking for the numbers before and after their own. And more and more people kept shoving in from behind. Olga Petrovna was tossed about like a chip. She unbuttoned her coat and wiped her forehead with her handkerchief.

Once she had caught her breath and was used to the semidarkness, Olga Petrovna also began to look for her

73

numbers: 343 and 345. 345 was a man, 343 a hunched-over, ancient woman.

"Your husband's Latvian, too?" the old woman asked, looking up at her with watery eyes.

"No, why?" replied Olga Petrovna in surprise. Why Latvian exactly? "My husband died a long time ago, but he was Russian."

"Tell me, please, do you already have a travel order?" Olga Petrovna was asked by the old Jewish woman with the silvery hair, the same one who had spoken to her on the embankment.

Olga Petrovna gave no answer. She simply couldn't understand what was going on here. The woman lying on the stairs, and now all sorts of stupid questions about Latvians, travel orders. . . . How did travel orders come into it? It seemed to her that she was not in Leningrad at all, but in some strange, alien city. It was strange to think that her office, the publishing house, was only half an hour's walk away. Natasha rattling on the typewriter . . .

Once they had found the numbers next to theirs the people stood quietly, waiting. Olga Petrovna could see now: the wooden staircase led up to a room which was also crowded with people, and it looked as if there was another room beyond that.

Olga Petrovna was furtively looking around her. There was a woman with a brief case, with woolen socks pulled on over her stockings and clumsy shoes—she was the same one who had been lying on the stairs. Here too people kept on coming up and speaking to her, but she wasn't taking down names any longer: it was too late.

To think that all these women were the mothers, wives and sisters of saboteurs, terrorists and spies! And the man—the husband or brother of one. They looked like perfectly ordinary people, just like in a streetcar or shop. Except that all looked tired and baggy-eyed. "I can imagine how terrible it must be for a mother to learn that her son is a saboteur," thought Olga Petrovna.

Now and again a woman would come down the narrow creaking stairs, pushing her way with difficulty through the crowd.

"Did they accept it?" she would be asked at the bottom.

"They accepted," and showed a pink slip.

But one of them—a milk woman, by appearance, carrying a large milk can—replied: "Deported!" and putting down her can, burst into loud sobbing, leaning her head against the doorpost. Her kerchief slipped down, showing her reddish hair and pretty little earrings.

"Quiet!" people shushed at her from all sides. "He doesn't like noise, he'll shut the window and that will be the end of that. Quiet!"

The milk woman straightened her kerchief and went out, tears rolling down her cheeks.

Olga Petrovna realized from what she heard people saying that most of these women had come to pass on money to husbands and sons who had been arrested, and some to find out whether a husband or son was here. Olga Petrovna's head was spinning from stuffiness and fatigue. She was very afraid that the mysterious little window they were all pushing toward would be shut before she got there.

"If it closes at two today we won't make it," the man said to her.

"At two? Must we really stand here till two?" thought Olga Petrovna miserably. "It can't be past ten yet!"

She closed her eyes, to try to stop her dizziness. There was a constant buzz of low, laconic conversation:

"When was yours picked up?"

75

"More than two months ago."

"Two weeks ago—mine."

"Tell me, do you know where else one can make enquiries?"

"At the prosecutor's office. But they don't tell you anything there."

"Have you been to Chaikovskaya Street? And Hertzen Street?"

"On Hertzen Street it's for the military."

"When was yours picked up?"

"It's my daughter."

"At Arsenalnaya Street, they say, clothing is accepted."

"You're what, Latvian?"

"No, we're Poles."

"When was yours picked up?"

"It's half a year already."

"What numbers have we reached?"

"Twenty something."

"Only? Good Lord, my God, let's hope he doesn't close at two! Last time he slammed the window shut at two sharp!"

Olga Petrovna rehearsed to herself what she was going to ask: "Had Kolya been brought to Leningrad? When could one see the judge—or, what was he called, the investigator? Couldn't it be today? And couldn't she have an interview with Kolya immediately?"

After two hours Olga Petrovna, following the old woman, reached the first step of the wooden staircase. In three hours she reached the first room. In four hours she was in the second room, and in five—following the winding line, she was back in the first room again. From behind she could make out the little wooden-framed window and, through the window, the broad shoulders and big hands of

76

a stout man. It was three o'clock. Olga Petrovna counted: there were fifty-nine people ahead of her.

The women, giving the name, timidly handed the money in at the window. The bandy-legged little boy was sobbing, and licking his tears away with his tongue. "Just wait till I have a talk with him," thought Olga Petrovna impatiently. "Let him take me at once to see the investigator, the prosecutor . . . or whoever it is. . . . How uncivilized things still are with us in some ways! It is so stuffy, they can't even ventilate the place. Someone ought to write a letter to *Leningrad Pravda* about it."

And then, finally, there were only three people left in front of Olga Petrovna. She also got some money ready, just in case. Kolya mustn't be caught short, meantime.

The bent-over old woman handed over thirty rubles at the window with a trembling hand, and received in return a pink slip. She peered at it with weak eyes.

Olga Petrovna quickly took the old woman's place. Behind the window she saw a stout young man with a puffy white face and sleepy little eyes.

"I would like to find out," began Olga Petrovna, bending down to see the face of the man behind the window better, "if my son is here. The point is that he was arrested by mistake. . . ."

"Last name?" the man interrupted.

"Lipatov. He was arrested by mistake, and for several days now I haven't known . . ."

"Just a moment, citizeness," said the man, bending over a drawer containing cards. "Lipatov or Lepatov?"

"Lipatov. I would like to go today to see the prosecutor or anyone you care to direct me to . . ."

"Letters?"

Olga Petrovna didn't understand.

77

"First name?"

"Oh, initials? N. F."

"N or M?"

"N, Nikolai."

"Lipatov, Nikolai Fyodorovich," the man read out, taking a card out of the drawer. "He's here."

"I would like to know . . ."

"We give no information. No more talk, citizeness. Next!"

Olga Petrovna hastily reached the thirty rubles through the window.

"Not allowed for him," the man said, pushing the bill aside. "Next! Move on, citizeness, don't get in the way."

"Go away," people whispered to Olga Petrovna from behind. "Or he'll slam the window."

Olga Petrovna reached home after five o'clock. She found Alik and Natasha in her room. She sank down on a chair and for several minutes didn't have the strength to take off her boots and coat. Alik and Natasha looked at her questioningly. She reported that Kolya was here, in prison, on Shpalernaya Street, but simply couldn't explain to them how it was she hadn't found out the cause of his arrest, or when she would be allowed to go and see him.

## TEN

Olga Petrovna took two weeks' leave from the publishers' without pay. While Kolya sat in prison, she simply couldn't think about all sorts of papers, or about Zoya Viktorovna! In any case, there wasn't time to go to the office, she had to stand in lines day and night.

She submitted her request to the lame Party organizer: after the arrest of Zakharov, he had been temporarily appointed acting director. He now sat in the office where Zakharov used to sit, behind the same large table with the telephones. He no longer wore a Russian shirt, but a gray suit from the Leningrad Clothing Store, with collar and tie—but he still looked insignificant.

Olga Petrovna explained that she needed the leave for domestic reasons. Timofeyev took a long time writing out a certificate in red ink. Without looking at Olga Petrovna, he then stated that she would be replaced this time by Zoya Vikotorovna, and ordered her to turn over her affairs to her.

"But why not Frolenko?" Olga Petrovna asked in surprise. "Zoya Viktorovna is not properly literate, and makes mistakes in spelling . . ."

Comrade Timofeyev made no reply, and stood up.

Oh well, what did it matter! Olga Petrovna left the room. She was hurrying to get in line.

All her days and nights now were spent neither at home nor at the office, but in some kind of a strange new world —in lines. She stood on the embankment of the Neva, or else on Chaikovskaya Street—there were benches there, one could sit down—or in the enormous hall of the Big House, or on the staircase in the prosecutor's office. She only went home to eat or sleep a little when Natasha or Alik replaced her in the line. (The director had given Alik permission to go to Leningrad for one week only, but he kept putting off his return to Sverdlovsk from day to day in the hope that he and Kolya would be able to return together.)

Olga Petrovna had learned a lot of things during those two weeks: she had learned that one should go at night to get on the list, at about eleven or midnight, and appear every two hours for the roll call, though it was better not to go away at all, or else one might be stricken off the list; that it was necessary to take a warm scarf and put on felt boots —otherwise, even when it was thawing, one's whole body would shiver with cold between three and six in the morning, and one's feet would freeze; she learned that the lists were taken away by the NKVD officials, and those who made out the lists were taken to the police station; that one must go to the prosecutor's office on the first day of the week, and there they received everyone, and not in alphabetical order—whereas on Shpalernaya Street the days for her letter were the seventh and twentieth (the first time she happened to hit her right day by some miracle); that the families of those who had been arrested were sent out of Leningrad—the "travel orders" were not a pass to a sanatorium but for deportation; that on Chaikovskaya Street information was given out by a red-faced old man with a bushy mustache like a cat's, and at the prosecutor's office by a young girl with a sharp nose and hair in tiny curls; that on Chaikovskaya Street you had to show your identification, on Shpalernaya Street—not. She learned that, among the unmasked enemies, there were a lot of Latvians and Poles—that explained why there were so many Latvian and Polish women in the lines. She was soon able to pick out at a glance which of the people in Chaikovskaya Street were not casual passers-by, but holding a place in line; even in the streetcar she could tell by their eyes which of the women were on their way to the iron gates of the prison. She became familiar with all the main and back stairs of the building along the embankment, and had no difficulty finding the woman with the list wherever she would hide. She knew now that, when she left home after a short sleep, wherever she went—on the street, on the staircase, in the corridors, the hall in Chaikovskaya Street, the embankment, the prosecutor's office—she would always find women, women and more women, old and young, in kerchiefs or in hats, alone or with children, or with babies, children crying from lack of sleep and frightened, silent women; and as in her childhood, after an excursion to the forest, when she closed her eyes tightly she saw nothing but berries, berries and more berries—so now, whenever she closed her eyes, she saw faces, faces, and more faces. . . .

81

But there was one thing she did not learn in the course of these two weeks: what had Kolya been arrested for? And who was going to try him, and when? And what was he accused of? And when would this stupid misunderstanding finally be over, and when would he return home?

At the information office on Chaikovskaya Street the red-faced old man with the bushy mustache would look at her identity papers and ask: "What is your son's name? You're his mother? Why doesn't his wife come? Not married? Lipatov, Nikolai? Being investigated," and throw the document back through the window; and before Olga Petrovna had time to open her mouth, the mechanical shutter would drop down with a bang and there would be a ring, meaning: "Next!" There was no point in talking to the shutter, so Olga Petrovna, after waiting a moment, would go away.

At the prosecutor's office the sharp-nosed young girl with the fine-curled hair would stick her head out of the window and rap out: "Lipatov? Nikolai Fyodorovich? The case has not yet reached the prosecutor's office. Inquire again in two weeks."

On Shpalernaya Street the stout, sleepy man invariably pushed aside her money, with the words: "Not allowed for him." That was all she knew about Kolya. Others were allowed money, but he for some reason was not. Why? But she understood already that to question the person behind the window was useless.

On the other hand, she would question Alik avidly about how it happened, how they took Kolya away.

And Alik would obediently recount again and again how they had been already asleep when suddenly there was a knock at the door and the dormitory manager came in, followed by the superintendent, and behind him someone in civilian clothes and another person in military uniform.

"What time was it?" Olga Petrovna would ask.

"Oh, about half-past one or so," Alik would reply and go on: "The superintendent turned on the light and the civilian asked: 'Which one here is Lipatov, Nikolai?' "

"Kolya was scared?" Olga Petrovna would interrupt with alarm.

"Not in the slightest," Alik would reply. "He dressed quickly and asked me to tell them at the plant the next day that he'd been detained by mistake, and that he might miss several days. . . . Let Motya Roitman take his place in the section—that's a Komsomol member who works there. . . ."

"And is it true he took nothing with him, absolutely nothing?" Olga Petrovna would anxiously clasp her hands.

Alik would explain that Kolya absolutely refused to take either a change of underwear or a towel, although the laundress had just brought the things back. " 'What for? I'll be back tomorrow or the day after.' 'I strongly advise you to take them,' said the military one with emphasis. But Kolya repeated to him too that there was no point, he'd be back tomorrow."

"That just shows what a clear conscience he had!" Olga Petrovna would cry, deeply moved. "But will they give him a towel there?"

Alik had waited patiently for Kolya, one day, two, three . . . it was not until the fourth day that he decided to go to Leningrad—to clear up the situation. He lied to the director about his mother being on the point of death. And the director—a goodhearted fellow—gave him permission to go.

Olga Petrovna would question Alik closely: perhaps Kolya had quarreled with the management? Been rude to someone? Associated with someone who later turned out to be a saboteur? Or some woman, perhaps, had entangled him in something?

"Oh, what woman, anyway?" Alik would answer with slight annoyance. "And anyway, can Nikolai be entangled? Surely you know him better than that? Our director used to say quite openly about him that this is a future world-famous engineer."

Yes, of course, of course, Kolya was not capable of doing anything wrong. She, Olga Petrovna, should certainly know what a heart of gold he had, and what a brain, and how absolutely loyal he was to the Soviet regime and the Party. But also, there is a reason for everything. Kolya was still young, and he had never been left on his own. He must have put someone's back up. You had to learn how to get along with people.

And Olga Petrovna looked at Alik with some hostility: he didn't take care of him properly. If only Kolya had remained in Leningrad, under his mother's eye, nothing would have happened to him. She should never have let him go to Sverdlovsk.

But even so, even so, nothing terrible could happen, Olga Petrovna went on persuading herself. Every hour, every minute, she expected Kolya to come home. On the way to get in line, she always left the key to her room on the shelf in the corridor, in the old usual place. She even left hot soup ready for him in the oven. And coming back, she hurried upstairs without pausing for breath, as she used to when expecting his letters; she'd enter the apartment and find Kolya there waiting for her, wondering where on earth his mother had gotten lost.

There had been a woman in the line last night who had said—Olga Petrovna heard her: "Return—just wait for him! Who winds up here doesn't return." Olga Petrovna wanted to interrupt but didn't want to get involved in it. In our country innocent people aren't held. Particularly Soviet patriots, like Kolya. They'll clear the matter up and let him out.

One evening Alik persuaded Olga Petrovna to lie down for an hour or so, then put on his jacket and scarf and said good-by. It was the nineteenth—he was going to get in line in Shpalernaya Street.

"I'll be there no later than two," said Olga Petrovna from her bed, in a weak voice.

"Olga Petrovna, even at five is all right," he retorted cheerfully, and went out the door.

Then for some reason he came back again. He went up to Natasha who was sitting beside the window, knitting.

"What do you think, Natalya Sergeyevna?" he asked, his bright eyes looking her straight in the face from behind his glasses, "there, in prison, are they all equally as guilty as Kolya? All those mothers standing in queues somehow look an awful lot like Olga Petrovna."

"I don't know," Natasha answered monosyllabically, in her new customary manner.

Natasha had never been talkative, but ever since Kolya had been arrested she scarcely spoke at all. In answer to questions she replied only: "Yes," "No," or "I don't know." Even if she'd been asked what her own name was, she'd probably only say, "I don't know." When not at the office she spent all her time with Olga Petrovna—cooking the dinner, washing the dishes, giving her water with valerian drops—or else standing in lines. And all the time she never opened her mouth.

"But, Alik," Olga Petrovna said quietly, "how can you even compare them? Kolya was arrested by mistake, whereas the others . . . Don't you read the papers, or what?"

"Uh! the papers . . ." said Alik, and left.

The papers had just published confessions made by the accused at their trials. In the line the day before Olga Petrovna had read a whole page over the shoulder of the man standing in front of her. Her legs were aching and her heart was heavy, but the paper was so interesting that she craned her neck and read the whole thing through. The accused gave all the details about the murders and poisonings and explosions—and Olga Petrovna shared the prosecutor's indignation.

"What are such things called?" the prosecutor would ask the accused with controlled anger. "Vile treachery," the accused replied contritely.

No, Olga Petrovna had been quite right to keep aloof from her neighbors in the line. She pitied them, of course, as human beings, pitied the children in particular; but still, an honest person should remember that all these women were the wives and mothers of prisoners, spies and murderers.

## ELEVEN

Two weeks passed. Alik returned to Sverdlovsk, to the plant; Olga Petrovna went back to work at the publishing house—still having found out nothing about Kolya.

The women in the line explained to her that the case would in all probability finally reach the prosecutor's office and when it reached the prosecutor's office she would be allowed to go and see the prosecutor. He received people not through a window, but behind a desk, and one could tell him everything.

For the moment there was only one thing to do—keep going to the office, count the lines, smile, distribute the work and, to the bang and clatter of the typewriters, go on constantly thinking of Kolya. Kolya sitting in prison, Kolya—in prison! Among bandits, spies and murderers. In a cell. Locked up.

Whenever she tried to visualize the prison and Kolya in it, she invariably thought of the picture of Princess Tarakanova! a dark wall, a girl with disheveled hair cowering, back against the dark wall, water flooding the cell, rats. . . . But in a Soviet prison, of course, it was not like that.

Alik, when he said good-by, advised her not to tell anyone about Kolya's arrest.

"I've no reason to be ashamed of Kolya . . ." began Olga Petrovna angrily, but then agreed with Alik: other people, after all, didn't know Kolya, and God knows what they might not imagine.

So she told no one, either at the office or in the apartment—only the policeman's wife, who found her one day weeping in the bathroom. The policeman's wife sighed sympathetically: "It's no use weeping—he may still return," she said consolingly. "I've noticed you, running around day and night, you're looking awful."

Five months had passed since the day of Kolya's arrest —winter had been followed by spring, spring by the stifling heat of June—and there was still no Kolya. Olga Petrovna was worn out by the heat, the waiting, and the nights spent in lines.

Five months, three weeks and four days . . . and five days . . . and six days.

Five months and four weeks . . . and Kolya had still not returned, money was still not allowed him, and Olga Petrovna suddenly began to have unpleasantnesses at work. One after another.

The person responsible for the unpleasantness was Zoya Viktorovna.

When Olga Petrovna returned to work after two weeks' leave, Zoya Viktorovna was left as her assistant: she had to check the typed manuscripts. Olga Petrovna knew that she was no help at all: she was illiterate herself! How was she to correct the mistakes of others? . . . But there was no going against Timofeyev's decision. So Zoya Viktorovna did the checking, and Olga Petrovna said nothing.

Then one day Comrade Timofeyev, rattling the keys —he now carried around with him all the keys to all the desks and all the rooms—stopped Olga Petrovna in the corridor and asked her to send Natasha to him after work. Olga Petrovna sent Natasha to his office and waited for her in the cloakroom, wondering what Comrade Timofeyev could want from Natasha.

Natasha came back fairly soon. Her pale face was impassive, only her lips seemed to tremble slightly.

"I've been dismissed," she said, when they went out into the street.

Olga Petrovna stopped short.

"Zoya Viktorovna showed the Party organizer the work I typed yesterday. You remember, the long article about the Red Army? I had written in one place Ret Army instead of Red."

"But wait a minute," Olga Petrovna was surprised, "that's a simple typing mistake. Why do you imagine you'll be dismissed tomorrow? Everyone knows you're the best typist in the office."

"He said: 'You will be dismissed for lack of vigilance.' "

Natasha walked straight ahead. The sun was beating straight into her face, but she didn't even lower her eyes.

Olga Petrovna took her home with her, and gave her tea. There was no Kolya. Before, when Kolya had been living happily in Sverdlovsk, Olga Petrovna hadn't been miserable because he wasn't with her; only a bit lonely. But now every object in the room seemed to be wailing to Olga Petrovna that Kolya was gone. On the window sill, all alone, stood his black cogwheel.

"I'll still come to the office tomorrow, but it will be the last time," said Natasha when saying good-by.

"Don't talk nonsense!" Olga Petrovna called after her. "That can't happen."

But it turned out that it could. On the next day the bulletin board in the corridor announced the dismissal of N. Frolenko and E. Gorskaya—the former secretary of the director. The reason given for the dismissal of Frolenko was lack of political vigilance; for that of the secretary, association with an unmasked enemy of the people, the former director Zakharov.

Next to this announcement was a large poster.

## NOTICE

Today at 5 P.M. there will take place a
### GENERAL MEETING
of all staff members of the publishing house.

### AGENDA:
1. Report by Comrade Timofeyev on sabotage activities on the publishing front.
2. Other business.

ATTENDANCE COMPULSORY!!!

Natasha took her brief case and left right after the bell rang, saying to everyone at once:—"Good-by!"—"Good luck!" replied the typists in unison; only Zoya Viktorovna said nothing: she was fixing her hair, looking at her reflection in the window pane.

90

Olga Petrovna, with a heavy heart, accompanied Natasha as far as the cloakroom: "Come over this evening," she whispered as she said good-by.

The chairman of the Mestkom was already summoning everyone to the director's office. The elevator woman, Marya Karpovna, was bringing in the chairs. Olga Petrovna went in and sat down in the front row. She felt frightened and alone. The ceiling light was switched on and the heavy blinds closed. The employees were coming in and taking their places. All their faces betrayed a kind of eager, anxious curiosity.

"Well, Comrades, do we have to send you a special invitation?" cried the chairman of the Mestkom, going into the editorial department.

Timofeyev stood at the table, concentrating on sorting out the papers.

The chairman declared the meeting open. She was unanimously elected, by a halfhearted show of hands, to preside over the meeting. Comrade Timofeyev cleared his throat.

"Comrades! We have met today to discuss an important matter," he began, "to take note of a criminal lack of vigilance in our publishing house and to consider jointly how to liquidate its consequences." This time he spoke smoothly and with confidence, almost without stammering. "For five whole years, under our very noses, so to speak, there operated in our community an individual now exposed as an enemy of the people, an evil bandit, a terrorist and a saboteur—former director Zakharov. Zakharov has now been deprived of the opportunity to do sabotage. But, in his time, he brought along with him a whole train of his puppets, his retinue, if I may put it like that, who built up a strong nest in our midst, and assisted him in all kinds of ways in the pursuit of his filthy Trotskyist machinations.

To the shame of our community, Zakharov's retinue has still not been liquidated. I have here in front of me"—he spread out the papers—"I have here documentary data which will give you documentary proof of their filthy counterrevolutionary activities."

Timofeyev paused and poured himself some water.

"What do these documents show?" he continued, wiping his mouth with the palm of his hand. "This document here contains irrefutable proof that, in the year nineteen hundred and thirty-two, on the personal order of the director, without consultation with the Mestkom and the personnel department, I repeat, on the personal order by the director, a certain N. Frolenko was hired."

Olga Petrovna shrank back, as though they had begun speaking about herself.

"And who is this Frolenko? She is—the daughter of a colonel, the proprietor of a so-called estate under the old regime. What, it is asked, was citizeness Frolenko doing in our publishing house, the daughter of an alien element, appointed by the bandit Zakharov? Another document will tell us about that. Under the wing of Zakharov, citizeness Frolenko learned to blacken our beloved Red Army of Workers and Peasants, to strike counterrevolutionary blows: she calls the Red Army the *Rat* Army. . . ."

Olga Petrovna felt her mouth go dry.

"And the former secretary Gorskaya? She was the director's loyal accomplice, on whom he could rely in all his, if I may say so, activity. How could it happen that this saboteur and his hangers-on were able, for five whole years, brazenly to bamboozle Soviet society? This, Comrades, can be explained by one thing only: the criminal relaxation of political vigilance."

Comrade Timofeyev sat down and began to drink some

water. Olga Petrovna longed for some water: her mouth and throat were so parched.

The chairman of the Mestkom rang the bell sharply, although all were silent and no one moved.

"Who wants to speak on the matter?" she asked.

Silence.

"Comrades, who asks for the floor?" the chairman asked again.

Silence.

"Could it really be that no one wants to say a few words on such a vital matter?"

Silence. Then suddenly, from the door, came a loud voice and all heads turned toward it.

It was the elevator woman, Marya Karpovna. Up till now she had not once spoken at a single meeting. Indeed, few people in the publishing house had ever heard her voice.

"Please, please, this way, Comrade Medvedeva!"

The elevator woman walked up to the table with heavy steps.

"Well, I too want to have my proletarian say in this. About that secretary, here, that is right, citizens. Like it used to be, she would get into the elevator in her galoshes, she would too leave her dirty footmarks all, all over, and you go and wipe up after her. Her making the mess and me wiping up. Take her up in the elevator, you do, and she even aims to be taken down by elevator too. And how can you refuse taking her down when she tries to get next to the director all the time. Where he goes, she goes too. He gets in the elevator, and she gets in the elevator after him. He gets in the car and she's sitting next to him in the car too. This is right that they worked hand in hand. . . . But every time I went to tell Comrade Timofeyev, in our own way, in plain proletarian language, how many times I reported to him: 'You stop her, the fine lady!' but he couldn't care less! Wouldn't pay any attention, just wave it off and walk away. You think, Comrade Timofeyev, the elevator woman is a little people, don't understand anything? You're mistaken! Today's not the old days any more! Under Soviet rule there are no little people—all are big."

"Quite right, Comrade Medvedeva, quite right," said Anna Grigorievna. "Does anyone else want to speak?"

Silence.

"May I please?" asked Olga Petrovna quietly. She stood up, then sat down again. "I only wanted to say a few words, about Frolenko. . . . Of course, it was dreadful, dreadful, what she wrote. But everyone can make mistakes in his work, isn't that true? She wrote not Red but Ret simply because, on the typewriter—as every typist knows—the letter *d* is near the letter *t*. Comrade Timofeyev said she wrote Rat, but she didn't, she wrote Ret, which is not quite the same thing. . . . There's nothing bad about it. A simple typing error. Frolenko is a highly qualified typist, and very conscientious. This was pure chance."

Olga Petrovna fell silent.

"Are you going to reply?" said the chairman of the Mestkom, turning to Timofeyev.

"Documents . . ." declared Timofeyev, rapping the papers with his knuckles. "You can't go against documents, Comrade Lipatov. Ret or Rat—it's all the same. An obvious act of class hostility on the part of citizeness Frolenko."

"Doesn't anyone else wish to speak? I declare the meeting closed."

The people dispersed quickly, hurrying home. From the cloakroom came a buzz of conversation: about number five streetcars running rarely, about the children's department in the Arcade getting in a consignment of excellent wool snow pants.

The accountant invited Zoya Viktorovna to go boating with him.

"You and your boating!" she scoffed, pouting her lips at the mirror as though to be kissed. "To go to the movies wouldn't be bad!"

About the meeting, or sabotage activities—not a word.

Olga Petrovna went quickly home, without even noticing the way. She had an idea that when she would get into her room and close the door, her head would stop aching, all this would end, and she would feel all right. Her temples were throbbing. Why was her head aching so? After all, it seemed that people hadn't been smoking at the meeting. Poor Natasha! She really had no luck! A first-class typist, and suddenly . . .

There was a note waiting for her at home:

"Dear Olga Petrovna! I've come back again. Motya Roitman reported me to the Komsomol, saying that I had associated with Nikolai. I have been expelled from the Komsomol seeing as how I refused to dissociate myself from Nikolai, and dismissed from work. It is very hard to be excluded from the ranks. I'll drop in tomorrow. See you soon! Yours, Aleksandr Finkelstein.

Olga Petrovna stood looking at the note. My God, so many unpleasantnesses all at once! First Kolya, then Natasha—and now Alik.

But Alik was probably at fault himself, he must have said something silly at some meeting there. He has become so short-tempered these days. The day he left, when she again asked him, tactfully, whether Kolya hadn't gotten into bad company there at Sverdlovsk, he had flushed scarlet and,

95

with his back against the wall, shouted at her: "Do you realize what you're saying, or don't you? Kolya's not guilty of anything, what's the matter with you—don't you believe it? You doubt it, or what?"

Of course he was not guilty of anything, there could be no question of it, but hadn't Kolya perhaps given some cause for offense? . . . And now Alik had probably said something insolent to his superiors at a meeting. Naturally he must stick up for Kolya—but somehow cautiously, tactfully, and in a restrained way. . . .

Olga Petrovna's head was aching. She felt as if the meeting were still going on. The voice of Timofeyev rang in her ears. She felt she couldn't breathe—as though Timofeyev's voice were constricting her. Should she lie down? No, that wouldn't do any good. She decided to take a bath.

There had been something about Timofeyev's words that had made her stiff with fear; perhaps if she took a bath, the feeling would pass. She went and got the wood from the cubbyhole herself and heated the water tank; Kolya used always to bring the wood for her, then Alik began getting it; and after Alik had gone back to Sverdlovsk for the second time—Natasha.

Oh, that Alik! Of course he was a good boy, and devoted to Kolya but he was so impetuous. One shouldn't be like that, blurting things out right from the shoulder. Wasn't it perhaps because of something he'd said that Kolya had been picked up? In the line once, on Shpalernaya Street, when she told Alik that they'd again refused to take the money for Kolya, he had burst out aloud, "Damned bureaucrats!" He might well have done something in Sverdlovsk, at the plant.

Olga Petrovna turned on the water, undressed and got into the bath—the wide white bathtub, bought by Fyodor

Ivanovich. She didn't feel like washing. She lay there, with her eyes closed. What would it be like at work now, without Natasha? And that Zoya Viktorovna! To think that there are such envious, malicious people in the world! Never mind, Natasha would find herself another job, somewhere not far away, and they would often see each other. . . . If only Kolya would return home soon! . . .

She looked at her hands, blurred by the water. Could it be that the secretary of the director was a saboteur? Better not to think about it. What a difficult day it had been! Thoughts of the meeting still oppressed her. She lay there with her eyes closed, in the peace and warmth.

In the kitchen, someone put out the primus stove, and the sound of voices and the clatter of dishes became immediately audible. The nurse was, as usual, being spiteful.

"I'm so far neither crazy nor blind," she was saying slowly. "I myself bought three liters of kerosene—two days ago. And there's only a drop left on the bottom—just enough to stuff up a dog's ass! Lately you can't leave anything in the kitchen."

"Who's going to take your kerosene?" came the low voice of the policeman's wife. One could hear by her voice that she was bending down, washing the floor perhaps, or stoking the stove. "We've all got enough kerosene of our own. Me, do you think?"

"It's not you I'm talking about. There are others than you living in the apartment. If one member of a family's in prison the rest are capable of anything. You don't get put in prison for good deeds."

Olga Petrovna's heart stopped beating.

"What if the son *is* in prison?" retorted the policeman's wife. "He'll sit for a while, and then they'll let him out. He's not a pickpocket of some kind, not a thief. A well-educated young man. All sorts of people get put in prison these days. My husband says lots of decent people are now being taken. But about this one, they even wrote in the paper. A famous shock worker."

"Some shock worker! Just masquerading," came Valya's voice.

"I suppose you think he's just an innocent little lamb!" The nurse was determined not to let the subject drop. "You will excuse me, but people in our country don't get locked up for nothing. Stop all your talk! Take me, they haven't locked me up, have they? And why? Because I'm an honest woman, a real Soviet citizen. . . ."

Olga Petrovna in the tub was seized by nervous shivering. Shaking as though in a fever, she dried herself, threw on her dressing gown, and tiptoed back into her room. She lay down under the blanket, and put a pillow on top, on her feet. But the shivering did not stop. She lay there trembling all over, staring ahead into the darkness.

About two o'clock at night, when everyone else was asleep, she got up, put on her coat, and made her way to the kitchen. She collected her kerosene can, her primus stove and her pots and took them all back with her to her room.

It was nearly morning before she fell asleep at last.

## TWELVE

The next day, Olga Petrovna found Alik waiting for her outside the publishing house. Without saying anything to her beforehand, so as not to upset her for nothing, he and Natasha had stood in line outside the prosecutor's office from early morning. Taking turns, they had waited for six hours, and the young lady at the window had told them half an hour ago that the case of Nikolai Lipatov was in the hands of the prosecutor Tsvetkov. They had then taken a place for Olga Petrovna in the line for the prosecutor Tsvetkov. Room Number Seven.

Alik tried to persuade Olga Petrovna to go home and have something to eat, but she was afraid to lose her place in the line and walked quickly, as fast as she could. She was on her way to save Kolya. His fate depended on what she was now about to say to the prosecutor. She hurried on, gasping for breath, rehearsing her speech as she went. She would tell the prosecutor how Kolya had joined the Komsomol as a boy, almost against his mother's wishes; how hard he had studied at school, and at the institute, how highly he was regarded at the plant, how he had been praised in *Pravda*, the central organ of the Party. He was a fine engineer, a loyal Komsomol member, a devoted son. How could a person like that possibly be suspected of sabotage or counterrevolution? What absurd nonsense, what a wild idea! She, his old mother, had come to testify to the judges that it was not true.

Alik opened the heavy door, and she went in.

Olga Petrovna had seen a lot of lines in the past few months, but never one like this. There were people standing, sitting and lying on every step, every landing and every ledge of the enormous staircase, going up five flights. It was impossible to go up it without stepping on someone's hand or foot.

The corridor near the window and near the door to Room Number Seven was jammed tight with people, like in a streetcar. These were the lucky ones, who had already been through waiting on the staircase. Natasha was standing hunched against the wall, under a poster proclaiming: "Up with the banner of revolutionary legality!" Having made their way to her, Olga Petrovna and Alik stopped and both took a deep breath. Alik took off his steam-clouded glasses and began to wipe them with his fingers.

"Well, I'll go now," Natasha announced right away. "You're behind this lady."

Olga Petrovna wanted to tell Natasha about yesterday's meeting, and how she had spoken up in her defense, but Natasha's head was already disappearing in the distance, near the stairs.

"Things are bad for Natalya Sergeyevna," Alik said. "They won't hire her anywhere. Like me."

He knew that Natasha had already applied to various places where typists were needed but when enquiries had been made at her previous place of work, she had been turned down everywhere. Alik too had applied to an engineering office right on the way from the station, but when they heard that he'd been expelled from the Komsomol, they wouldn't even talk to him.

"We've been put on the black list as I understand it. Scoundrels! How is it there are suddenly so many dirty swine around?" Alik burst out in a rage.

"Alik!" exclaimed Olga Petrovna reprovingly. "How can you talk like that? It's for using words like that that they expelled you from the Komsomol."

"It wasn't for sharp words, Olga Petrovna." Alik was offended, and his lips started trembling. "It was because I refused to renounce Nikolai."

"No, no, Alik," Olga Petrovna protested gently, touching his sleeve. "You're still very young, I assure you, you're wrong. It's all a matter of being tactful. I, for instance, at the meeting yesterday defended Natalya Sergeyevna. And you see? Nothing happened to me. Believe me, this business with Kolya is a nightmare to me. I'm his mother. But I realize it's a temporary misunderstanding, extreme exaggeration, disagreements. . . . One has to be patient. And you start right away: scoundrels! Swine! Remember what Kolya always said—we still have a lot of imperfection, and a lot of red tape."

Alik said nothing. His face had frozen in a stubborn, obstinate expression. He was unshaven and looked pinched. There were dark marks under his eyes. And his eyes looked different from under the glasses—fixed and gloomy.

101

"I have already sent a petition to the district committee. If they don't reinstate me, I'll go to Moscow. Straight to the Central Committee of the Komsomol," he declared.

"Poor lad!" thought Olga Petrovna. "He's going to have a hard time while out of work. His aunt is probably already reproaching him." And Olga Petrovna, bending toward Alik, whispered:

"When they release Kolya you'll be reinstated at once." And smiled at him.

But Alik did not return her smile.

It was still a long way to the prosecutor's door.

Olga Petrovna counted about forty people. They went in two at a time—there were two prosecutors interviewing people in room Number Seven, not one—but even so, the line moved slowly.

Olga Petrovna examined the faces around her: it seemed to her that she had seen most of those women before—on Shpalernaya or Chaikovskaya Street, or here at the prosecutor's office; maybe these were the same, or perhaps they were different ones. All the women standing in the lines outside the prison had something similar about their faces: they looked tired, resigned, somehow secretive. Many of them were holding white slips—Olga Petrovna knew they were deportation "vouchers." Here in the line, three questions were heard all the time: "Where are you going?" or "When do you go?" or "Have you had a confiscation?"

Olga Petrovna leaned against the wall and closed her eyes for a moment. What a heartless, malicious, stupid woman that accountant's wife was! To imagine that Kolya was a saboteur! Why, she'd known him since childhood! Olga Petrovna would never, never set foot in the kitchen again. Until that woman begged her forgiveness. Just imagine how ashamed she'd be when Kolya returned! Olga

Petrovna would tell Kolya everything—about what marvelous friends Natasha and Alik were (without them she simply couldn't have coped with the lines) and about that snake, the nurse. Let him realize what harpies there were in the world!

When she opened her eyes, Olga Petrovna noticed a little girl crouching down against the wall. She was wearing a coat, buttoned all the way up. "How people bundle children up nowadays," thought Olga Petrovna, "even in summer." Then suddenly she recognized the girl: it was the little daughter of the director, Zakharov. The child was fidgeting about by the wall, sniveling and whining from the heat. And the tall, slender woman in the light-colored suit—the one Olga Petrovna and Alik had been standing behind for the past hour—must be the director's wife. Yes, of course it was.

"How's your trumpet, not broken yet?" Olga asked tenderly, bending down over the child. "Or have you torn the tassel off already? Do you remember me? At the New Year's tree? Let me unbutton your collar for you."

The child was silent, looking at Olga Petrovna with round eyes, and jerking her mother's hand.

"What's the matter? Answer the lady!" the director's wife urged the child.

"I knew your husband." Olga Petrovna turned to her. "I work in the publishing house."

"Ah!" drawled the director's wife, twisting her lips painfully. She wore lipstick but it was applied beyond the outline of the lips themselves. A beautiful woman, no doubt about that—but Olga Petrovna no longer found her as young and elegant as she had been six months before, when she used to stop in at the office to see her husband, and returned bows graciously to the staff in the corridor.

"What's happened about your husband?" enquired Olga Petrovna.

"Ten years at remote camps."

"Then he was guilty after all. I would never have believed it. Such a nice person," thought Olga Petrovna.

"And they're sending her and me to Kazakhstan, to some village or mountain hamlet, or something. . . . We're off tomorrow. I'll starve to death out there, without work."

She spoke in a loud, sharp voice, and everyone turned to glance at her.

"And where's your husband been sent?" asked Olga Petrovna in order to change the subject.

"How should I know? Would they tell you where?"

"But then how will you . . . in ten years . . . when he's released . . . how will you find each other? You won't know his address, and he won't know yours."

"And do you imagine," asked the director's wife, "that any one of them"—and she gestured at the crowd of women with the "travel vouchers"—"knows where her husband is? The husbands have already been taken away, or will be taken away tomorrow, or today; the wives too are sent off to some hell-hole, and haven't the foggiest idea how they're going to find their husbands later. How should I know? No one knows, and I don't either."

"You have to persist," replied Olga Petrovna quietly. "If they won't tell you here, you have to write to Moscow. Or else, what's going to happen? You are going to lose sight of one another completely."

The director's wife looked her up and down.

"Who is it? Your husband? Your son?" she asked, so viciously that Olga Petrovna involuntarily drew back closer to Alik. "All right then, when they send your son away, you just be persistent, go and find out where he is."

"My son won't be sent away," said Olga Petrovna apologetically. "You see, he's not guilty. He was arrested by mistake."

"Ha-ha-ha!" the director's wife burst out laughing, carefully enunciating the syllables. "Ha! ha! ha! By mistake indeed!" And suddenly tears poured from her eyes. "Here, you know, everything's by mistake. . . . Oh! stand still, can't you!" she shouted at the child and bent down to her in order to hide her tears.

There were now five people between Olga Petrovna and the door. Olga Petrovna repeated to herself the words she was going to say to the prosecutor. She thought with condescending pity about the director's wife: "That's husbands for you! It's they who make trouble, and their wives suffer for it. She's now going to Kazakhstan, with the child, and all these lines, too—it's enough to make anyone a nervous wreck!"

"Listen, I'll go in with you," suggested Alik suddenly. "As a colleague and friend. I shall tell the Comrade Prosecutor that in Nikolai we had an absolutely pure and honest man, an indomitable Bolshevik. I shall tell him about how our plant adopted the use of the Fellows' cogwheel cutter, which we owe exclusively to the inventiveness of Nikolai."

But Olga Petrovna did not want Alik to go to the prosecutor. She was afraid of his impetuosity: he'd say something insolent, and ruin everything. No, she would do better to go alone. She assured Alik that the prosecutor only received relatives.

At last her turn came. The director's wife opened the door and entered. Olga Petrovna, with sinking heart, followed her in.

Near the wall, on either side of the dark, empty room, were two desks, each with a tattered armchair in front of it.

Behind the table on the right sat a plump, white-faced man with china-blue eyes. Behind the one on the left, a hunchback. The director's wife and little girl went up to the white-faced man, Olga Petrovna to the hunchback. She had long ago heard in the lines that the prosecutor Tsvetkov was a hunchback.

Tsvetkov was speaking on the telephone. Olga Petrovna sank down into the chair.

The prosecutor Tsvetkov was short and thin, and dressed in a greasy navy-blue suit. He had a pointed little head and a large, round hump. A growth of black hair covered his long wrists and the backs of his fingers. The way he held the telephone receiver was not human but somehow ape-like. Altogether, he looked so much like an ape to Olga Petrovna that she found herself thinking: "If he wanted to scratch behind his ear—he'd no doubt use his foot."

"Dubinin?" shouted Tsvetkov hoarsely into the telephone. "Tsvetkov here. Hello! Tell Rudnev that I've already checked everything. Let him send it. What's that? I said—let him send it."

At the other table the plump, white-faced man with the blue, doll-like eyes and the small, plump, female hands, was talking politely with the director's wife.

"I want you to change me over from a village to a city of some sort," she was saying in a jerky voice, standing in front of the table and holding the little girl by the hand. "In a village I'll be without work. I shall have nothing to feed myself and my child on. I am a stenographer. In a village there's no stenographic work to be done. I ask you please to send me not to a village, but to some city—even one in that what do you call it?—Kazakhstan."

"Kindly take a seat, citizeness," the white-faced man invited her politely.

"What do you want?" Tsvetkov asked Olga Petrovna, putting down the receiver and glancing at her with his little black eyes.

"It's about my son. His name's Lipatov. He was arrested through a misunderstanding, by mistake. I was told you were handling his case."

"Lipatov?" repeated Tsvetkov, pausing to recollect. "Ten years of remote camps." And he took up the receiver again. "Section A? 244-16."

"What? He's already been tried?" exclaimed Olga Petrovna.

"244-16? Call Morozova."

Olga Petrovna fell silent, her hand on her heart. She felt her heart thumping slowly, infrequently and loudly. The throbbing resounded in her temples and her ears. Olga Petrovna decided to wait until Tsvetkov finally finished speaking on the telephone. She looked in terror at his long, hairy wrists, his hump covered with dandruff, his unshaven, yellow face. Patience, patience! And again she felt her heart throbbing, in her temples and her ears.

At the opposite table the white-faced prosecutor was speaking softly to the director's wife.

"There's no need for you to get upset, citizeness. Take a seat, please do. It is my duty, as the representative of legality, to remind you that the great Stalin constitution guarantees everyone, without distinction, the right to work. Since no one is depriving you of any civil rights you continue to enjoy the right to work, wherever you may be living."

The director's wife stood up quickly and went toward the door. The little girl ran after her with small, unsteady steps.

"You still here? What do you want?" snarled Tsvetkov, at last putting down the receiver.

"I would like to know what my son could have been guilty of," replied Olga Petrovna, making a supreme effort to prevent her voice from trembling. "He has always been an irreproachable Komsomol member, and a loyal citizen . . ."

"Your son has confessed to his crimes. The investigation is in possession of his signature. He was a terrorist and took part in terrorist activity. Understand?"

Tsvetkov sat there opening and shutting the drawers of the desk. Pulling them out and slamming them shut. The drawers were empty.

Olga Petrovna tried desperately to remember: what else was it she wanted to say? But everything had gone out of her mind. In that room, and with a person like that, anyway, all words were of no avail. She stood up and made her way to the door.

"How can I find out now where he is?" she asked from the door.

"That does not concern me."

In the corridor, Alik was loyally waiting for her. Silently they squeezed their way through the crowd in the corridor, and then down the stairs. Silently they went out into the street. In the street, the streetcar bells clanged, the sun shone brightly, passers-by pushed each other. The hot, stuffy summer day was still far from over.

"Well, what, Olga Petrovna, what?" asked Alik anxiously.

"Sentenced. To remote camps. For ten years."

"You're joking!" gasped Alik. "Whatever for?"

"Taking part in terrorist activity."

"Kolya—in terrorist activities? Raving nonsense!"

"The prosecutor says he himself confessed. The investigation is in possession of his signature."

Tears were pouring down Olga Petrovna's cheeks. She stopped, clutching a protruding part of the wall.

"Kolya Lipatov—a terrorist!" Alik was choking with indignation. "What scum they are, what utter scum! Why, it's fantastic nonsense! You know what, Olga Petrovna, I'm beginning to think all this is some colossal plot. The saboteurs have gotten themselves into the NKVD—and are running the show. They are themselves enemies of the people!"

"But Kolya confessed, Alik, he confessed, you understand, Alik, you understand . . ." sobbed Olga Petrovna.

Alik took Olga Petrovna firmly by the arm and led her home. Outside the door of the apartment, while she was searching in her bag for the key, he began again:

"Kolya had nothing to confess to, surely you can't doubt that, can you? I don't understand anything any more, I understand nothing. There's only one thing I'd like now: to talk to Comrade Stalin, face to face. Let him explain to me what he thinks about all this!"

## THIRTEEN

Olga Petrovna lay awake all night, without even closing her eyes. How many nights had it been now since Kolya's arrest? Endless, interminable nights! She knew it all by heart already: the summer sound of feet under the window, the shouts from the beer hall next door, the rumble of streetcars dying out, then a short silence, and darkness—and then again the pale light filtering into the room, and another day beginning, a day without Kolya.

Where was Kolya now? What was he sleeping on? What was he thinking about? Where was he? With whom? Olga Petrovna never for a moment doubted his innocence: terrorist activity? Raving nonsense—as Alik said. He must have come up against an overzealous investigator who confused him and made him lose his head. And Kolya wasn't able to clear himself, he was still very young, after all.

Toward morning, when it was beginning to get light

again, Olga Petrovna at last remembered the word she had been trying to think of all night: alibi. She had read about it somewhere. He had simply been unable to produce an alibi.

During the first hours at the office she seemed to feel a little better somehow. The sun was shining brightly, the dust dancing in the sunbeams, and the typewriters were clattering busily. In the lunch hour the typists all ran down into the street, then sucked ice cream on sticks endlessly. It was all so familiar. . . . But Kolya had been condemned —and to ten years! Now, in the light of day, it became clear what rubbish this all was! She wouldn't see Kolya for ten years. But why not? What hideous nonsense! It simply couldn't be. One fine day—very soon—things would return to normal again: Kolya would be at home, arguing again with Alik as usual, about cars and locomotives, drawing plans again—only now she would not let him go to Sverdlovsk no matter what. There were jobs available in Leningrad, too.

During lunch hour she went out into the corridor to stretch her legs; she was afraid of falling asleep sitting down. In the corridor the staff were crowding in front of a new wall newspaper, a large special issue with headings in red letters and the portraits of Lenin and Stalin one on either side of the title, written in large bright-red letters.

## "OUR WAY"

Olga Petrovna went up to the newspaper.

How was it possible that saboteurs were able for five whole years to engage in their filthy activities with impunity under the very nose of Soviet society?

she read. It was the editorial by Timofeyev.

112

In the next column was the beginning of an article by the chairman of the Mestkom. Anna Grigorievna made a caustic attack on Timofeyev on the grounds that his speech at the meeting had not contained sufficient self-criticism. If society had allowed sabotage activities to pass unnoticed, the one first responsible for it must be Comrade Timofeyev, the former Party organizer. Especially since, as it now became clear, the Party organizer had received timely warnings from below: warning had been given by Comrade Medvedeva, who had long ago smelled out the director's secretary with her proletarian sense.

Olga Petrovna cast her eyes over the next column. And before she grasped the meaning of what she was reading, she suddenly flushed hot inside. The article was about her, about Olga Petrovna, about how she had spoken in defense of Natasha. The author, whose identity was concealed by the initial X, wrote:

A scandalous occurrence took place at the meeting, for which, in our opinion, insufficient raps over the knuckles have been administered. Comrade Lipatova came out with a real defense speech—and whom did she deem it necessary to defend? Frolenko, a colonel's daughter, who had permitted herself a gross anti-Soviet jibe at our beloved Red Army of Workers and Peasants. It is known that Comrade Lipatova constantly favored Frolenko, gave her overtime work, went to the movies with her, and so on, etc. At present, when the publishing house is about to enlist all the efforts of honest workers and of Party and non-Party Bolsheviks in order to liquidate with all possible speed the consequences of the "management" by Kuzmin—Zakharov and Co.—is it permissible, at this crucial moment to retain such persons on the staff of our publishing house? Up with the banner of Bolshevik vigilance, as we are taught by the genius of the leader of the peoples,

Comrade Stalin! Let us root out all saboteurs, both secret and open, together with all those in sympathy with them!

## X

The bell rang, signifying the end of the lunch hour. Olga Petrovna went back to her office. How was it she hadn't noticed before that everyone was looking at her in a peculiar way today?

Back at home, she buried her head in her pillow—her last refuge. And sleep immediately closed her eyes for her.

She slept a long time and dreamed about Kolya. He was wearing a fluffy gray sweater. There were skates attached to his boots. And then, bending low, he began skating along the corridor of the publishing house.

When she woke up, the blue of dusk was already falling outside, but the light was on in her room. Natasha was sitting at the table sewing. It was obvious she had already been sewing there for a long time.

"Come and sit here, nearer me," said Olga Petrovna, in a faint voice, licking the taste of daytime sleep from her lips.

Natasha quietly brought over her chair, and sat down near the head of the bed.

"You know, Kolya's been sentenced, to ten years. Alik has no doubt already told you."

Natasha nodded.

"Oh, yes, you know?" Olga Petrovna remembered. "They wrote about me in the wall newspaper, claiming that I defend saboteurs and that there was no place for me in the publishing house."

Natasha raised her head slowly:

"Alik has been arrested. Last night . . ."

## FOURTEEN

If Olga Petrovna didn't sleep at night, it made no difference to her what time of day or night it was. The light hurt her eyes, her legs ached and there was a gnawing feeling in her heart. But when she did manage to sleep at night, the worst moment, without any doubt, was just after she woke up. When she opened her eyes and caught sight of the window, the bottom of the bed, her dress hanging over the chair—for a moment she thought of nothing but these objects. She recognized them: window, chair, dress. But the next moment—somewhere in the region of the heart, she was seized by a feeling of dread, like a pain, and through the haze of that pain she would suddenly remember everything: Kolya had been condemned to ten years, Natasha had been fired, Alik arrested, and about her they had written that she was hand in glove with saboteurs. Yes, and also—the kerosene.

At the office she no longer spoke to anyone. Even the papers brought to her for typing she placed before the typists without a word. And no one spoke to her either. From behind her desk in the office, she scrutinized the faces of the typists, trying to guess who had written about her in the paper. Most likely Zoya Viktorovna. But was she able to write so smoothly? And when could she have seen her and Natasha at the movies together? They hadn't seen her even once.

Loitering wretchedly in the corridor one day she nearly ran into Natasha. Natasha looked like a sleepwalker, picking her way carefully as though in darkness.

"Natasha, you here?" cried Olga Petrovna in surprise.

"I've read the paper. Don't speak to me. They'll see!" whispered Natasha quickly.

That evening she visited Olga Petrovna. Now she seemed to be excited and talked incessantly, jumping from one subject to another. Olga Petrovna had never before heard Natasha talk so much. And this time she was not embroidering or sewing.

"What do you think, is Kolya still here in the city, or far away already?" she asked suddenly.

"I don't know, Natasha," Olga Petrovna replied with a sigh. "On Shpalernaya Street it's the nineteenth for his letter, L, and today it's only the tenth."

"No, I don't mean that. What feeling have you about it?" Natasha made a gesture in the air. "Is he still here, near us, or a long way off already? I think he's a long way off. I suddenly had a feeling yesterday: he's far away already. He's no longer here. . . . And, you know, Olga Petrovna, the elevator woman refused to take me up. 'I'm

116

not obliged to take up all kinds. . . .' Yes, Olga Petrovna, you simply must get out of the office at once, tomorrow. Promise me you'll leave. Please promise it, my dear! Tomorrow—all right?"

Natasha knelt on the couch where Olga Petrovna was sitting, her hands entreatingly clasped.

Then she sat down at the table, seized a pen and herself composed a letter of resignation in the name of Olga Petrovna. She assured Olga Petrovna that it was absolutely essential for her to resign voluntarily—otherwise she'd most certainly be dismissed for associating with saboteurs —"That's with me." Natasha's pale lips smiled. And then no one would hire her for any job for any reason.

Olga Petrovna signed the resignation. She'd already thought of leaving herself. Things had becoming terrifying, somehow, at the office. The very sight of Timofeyev limping along with the bunch of keys in his hand sent cold shivers down her back.

"In any case I won't be able to work in Leningrad," she said sadly. "I shall be deported anyway. All wives and mothers get sent away."

"What do you think?" asked Natasha, taking a book off the shelf and then replacing it immediately. "What's the explanation for the fact that Kolya confessed? Of course a person can be tripped up, confused, that I understand—but only in small things. But how can Kolya have been reduced to such a state that he confessed to a crime which he never committed? That I simply cannot understand. And why do they all confess? All the wives are told that their husbands have confessed. They've all been confused."

"He simply wasn't able to establish his alibi," explained Olga Petrovna. "You're forgetting, Natasha, he's still very young."

"And why has Alik been arrested?"

"Oh, Natasha, if only you knew what rude things he's been saying in front of everyone in the lines. I am now convinced that his tongue was the undoing of Kolya, too."

Natasha was getting ready to leave. As she said good-by, she suddenly embraced Olga Petrovna.

"What's the matter with you today?" Olga Petrovna asked her in surprise.

"Nothing . . . don't get up, please don't. How like Kolya you look, or rather, how much Kolya resembles you. . . . You'll hand in your letter of resignation tomorrow, won't you? You won't change your mind?" she asked, looking Olga Petrovna straight in the eye. "And then don't forget, the thirtieth is the letter F, some money simply must be transmitted to Alik, he hadn't a penny on him, and his aunt will be too scared to pass any over. . . . And another thing, my dear, I beseech you, please go and see a doctor. I beg of you! You're looking like death!"

"What's the use of a doctor . . . it's Kolya!" muttered Olga Petrovna miserably, and lowered her eyes full of tears.

Next morning she went straight to the director's office and wordlessly laid her resignation on the glass-topped table. Timofeyev read it through and nodded, also without a word.

All the formalities were completed with remarkable speed. Two hours later the announcement of her resignation was already posted on the wall. And three hours later, the polite accountant had already handed her the final wages.

"So you're leaving? Ai-ai-ai, that's bad! Mind you come and see us, you mustn't forget your old friends."

For the last time, she went along the corridor.

"Good-by," she said to the typists, when the bell had rung and they were already banging down the lids of their Underwoods.

"All the best!" they all called out in chorus, just as they had done to Natasha not long ago; and one of them even came up and firmly shook Olga Petrovna's hand. Olga Petrovna was very touched: what a courageous, noble girl that was!

"Good luck!" sang out Zoya Viktorovna gaily, and suddenly the suspicion that had been tormenting her became an absolute certainty—it was Zoya Viktorovna who had written that article, she and no one else!

She went out into the street, into the din of the summer day. The sun was scorching down. No more going to the office—that was finished forever.

She had meant to go home, but then decided to call on Natasha instead. On all the street corners were small boys holding out bunches of bluebells and daisies with their sweaty fingers. Everything was just as usual, even flowers were sold. But because Kolya was sitting in prison or being taken somewhere to the rumble of wheels—the whole world became senseless and incomprehensible.

Climbing slowly up to the fifth floor—God, how climbing stairs was becoming more and more difficult every day!—she rang the bell. The door was opened by Natasha's neighbor; she was wearing an apron, and drying her hands on it.

"Natalya Sergeyevna was taken to hospital this morning," the woman said in a loud whisper. "Poisoned herself. With veronal. Mechnikov hospital."

Olga Petrovna backed away from her. The woman slammed the door.

Number seventeen streetcar was a long time coming.

119

Two number nines passed, and two twenty-twos, and still no seventeen. . . . But there it appeared at last, stopped, and then trundled slowly on again, wearily, stopping at every traffic light. Olga Petrovna stood. All the seats reserved for people with children were taken, and when a ninth woman with a baby got on no one was willing to give up his seat to her.

"They'll soon be filling up the whole streetcar!" shouted an old woman with a stick. "They ride back and forth. We in our time used to carry our children in our arms, just you hold it, it won't kill you."

Olga Petrovna's knees were shaking, from fright, from the heat, from the old woman's vicious shouting. At last she got off. She was certain, for some reason, that Natasha was already dead.

The hospital glittered toward her with all its clean-washed windows. She entered the cool vestibule.

In front of the enquiries window was a line of three people. Olga Petrovna did not dare to walk straight up to the head of the line. Enquiries were answered by a pretty nurse in a starched white uniform. Near her, in front of the telephone, was a bunch of bluebells in a glass.

"Hello, hello!" she shouted into the telephone after listening to Olga Petrovna's enquiry. "Second therapeutical ward?" Then, putting down the receiver, she said, "Frolenko, Natalya Sergeyevna, died at four o'clock this afternoon, without regaining consciousness. Are you a relative? You may have a pass for admission to the mortuary."

## FIFTEEN

O n the evening of the eighteenth, Olga Petrovna put on her autumn coat with a scarf under it, and her galoshes, got in line on the embankment. For the first time she had to stand all night through. Who could relieve her now? Neither Natasha nor Alik was there any longer.

Olga Petrovna had accompanied Natasha's pine coffin through the entire city to the cemetery. It was raining for a long time that day, and the great wheels of the horse-drawn hearse splashed mud into her face.

Natasha was lying in her grave, in the yellow earth, not far from Fyodor Ivanovich. But where were Alik and Kolya? This was impossible to understand.

She stood on the embankment the whole night through, leaning against the cold parapet. Cold damp rose from the

Neva. For the first time in her life Olga Petrovna saw the sun rise here. It rose from somewhere beyond Okha, and the surface of the river was suddenly swept by tiny waves, as though it were being rubbed against the grain.

Toward morning, Olga Petrovna's legs went numb from fatigue, she had no feeling in them at all and when, at nine o'clock, the crowd rushed toward the prison door, Olga Petrovna was incapable of running: her legs were heavy and she felt as though she had to lift them up with her hands to make them move at all.

Her number this time was fifty-three. Two hours later she reached the window, reached in with the money and gave the name. The stout, sleepy-looking man looked at some kind of card and then, instead of the usual "not allowed for him," answered "deported." Since the interview with Tsvetkov, Olga Petrovna had been fully prepared for this answer, but it stunned her nonetheless.

"Where to?" she asked distractedly.

"He'll write to you himself. . . . Next!"

She went home on foot—standing about waiting for a streetcar was more tiring than walking. It was hot and dusty, she unbuttoned her heavy coat and untied her scarf. The passers-by seemed to have forgotten how to walk straight: they kept on bumping into her on all sides.

Kolya would write to her. She'd receive a letter from him again, as she used to from Sverdlovsk.

Olga Petrovna now spent all her days looking for work, starting off early in the morning, without getting breakfast or even making her bed. The papers carried many notices: "Typist wanted." Her legs felt like lead, but she went around, patiently, all day, answering all advertisements.

They asked the same question everywhere she went:

"Have you anyone who's been repressed?"

The first time she didn't understand.

"Relatives arrested," they explained.

She was afraid to lie.

"My son," she replied.

It then turned out that there were no vacancies on the staff.

And there was no vacancy anywhere for Olga Petrovna.

She was now afraid of everything and everyone. She was afraid of the janitor, whose indifference was, she felt, tinged with grimness. She was afraid of the house manager, who no longer nodded good day to her (she had ceased to be apartment representative; the accountant's wife had been elected to replace her). She was deadly afraid of the accountant's wife. She was afraid of Valya. She was afraid to walk past the publishing house. Returning home after her fruitless search for a job, she was afraid of finding a summons from the police awaiting her. Perhaps the police would summon her in order to take her identity papers away, and deport her? She was afraid of every ring of the bell: perhaps they'd come to seize her possessions?

She was afraid to go and hand over money for Alik. On the evening before the thirtieth, as she arrived at the line, Kiparisova came up to her. Kiparisova came to the line almost every day, and not on her day only, in order to find out from the women there what news there was: who had already been deported, who was still here, whether the timetable had been changed by any chance.

"You shouldn't be doing this, not at all!" Kiparisova whispered in Olga Petrovna's ear, when the latter told her what she'd come for. "They'll tie up your son's case with that of his friend—and things will turn out badly: Article

123

fifty-eight, paragraph eleven—counterrevolutionary organization. . . . What do you need to do that for, I don't understand!"

"But they don't ask there who is handing over the money," Olga Petrovna pointed out timidly. "They only ask who it's for."

Kiparisova took her by the arm and led her away from the people.

"They don't need to ask," she said in a whisper. "They know everything." Her eyes were huge, black, sleepless.

Olga Petrovna returned home.

The next day she didn't get up from her bed. There was no longer anything to get up for. She had no desire to dress, put on her stockings or put her feet to the floor. What did it matter to her if the room was in a mess, what did she care about the dust? Let it be!

She didn't even feel hungry. She lay in bed thinking of nothing, reading nothing. Novels had long since ceased to entertain her: she was incapable of breaking away from her life for even an instant and concentrating on anyone else's. The newspapers filled her with vague terror: all the words in them were like in that article in the wall newspaper *Our Way*.

Now and again she pushed off the blanket and looked down at her legs: they were huge and swollen as if they'd been filled with water.

When the light on the wall faded and evening was approaching, she remembered about Natasha's letter. It was still lying under her pillow. Olga Petrovna wanted to read it again, and propping herself up on her elbow, she drew it out of the envelope:

Dear Olga Petrovna! [Natasha wrote in farewell] You mustn't weep for me, no one needs me, anyway. For me

124

it's better like this. Maybe everything will turn out all right, and Kolya will come home, but I haven't the strength to wait for that. I can't make sense of the present phase of the Soviet regime. But you must go on living, my dear one, the time will come when it will be possible to send him parcels, and he will need you. Send him canned crab, he used to like it. Thank you for everything and for what you said about me at the meeting. I am sorry for you, about what you have suffered because of me. You will have my tablecloth to remind you always of me. How we used to go to the movies together—you remember? When Kolya returns, put it on his table, the colors on it are bright and cheerful. Tell him I never believed anything bad about him.

Olga Petrovna put the letter back under her pillow again.

"Perhaps I should tear it up. She writes about the present phase of the Soviet regime. Suppose they find the letter? Then they'll connect Kolya's case with Natasha's. . . . Or perhaps I should keep it? . . . Natasha's already dead, anyway."

## SIXTEEN

Three months went by, and then another three, and winter came. January—the anniversary of Kolya's arrest. In a few months it would be the anniversary of Alik's arrest and, immediately afterward, the anniversary of Natasha's death.

On the anniversary of Natasha's death, Olga Petrovna would go visit her grave. But on the anniversary of Kolya's arrest there was nowhere for her to go. Who knew where he was?

No letter came from Kolya. Olga Petrovna looked into the mailbox five, ten times a day. Sometimes there were newspapers for the accountant's wife or post cards for Valya—from her numerous admirers—but never a letter for Olga Petrovna.

This was the second year now that she did not know

where he was, or how he was. Had he died? Could she have ever imagined that a time would come when she wouldn't even know whether Kolya was dead or alive?

She was already working again. It was only Koltsov's article in *Pravda* that had saved her from dying of starvation. A few days after the publication of that article—a remarkable article about slanderers and opportunists harming honest Soviet people for nothing—Olga Petrovna was taken on to work at a library: not on the permanent staff, though, only on a temporary basis. But still, they did hire her. Her job was to write out cards for the catalogue, in a special librarian's script: four hours a day, a hundred and twenty rubles a month.

At her new place of work, Olga Petrovna not only talked to no one, she didn't even say good morning, or good-by. Bending over the table piled high with books, her short gray hair falling down over her glasses, she sat out her four hours; then she got up, arranged the cards in a stack, took her rubber-tipped cane which always stood beside her chair, locked the cards up in the bookcase and slowly, without a glance at anyone, went away.

There was a whole pile of canned crab already rising on the window sill in Olga Petrovna's room, and grains of buckwheat crunched underfoot; but still Olga Petrovna went to the food shops every day after work, buying up more and more provisions. She bought canned food, rendered butter, dried apples, lard—there was plenty of all these things in the shop but by the time Kolya's letter came they might well have suddenly disappeared.

Early in the morning sometimes, even before going to work, Olga Petrovna wandered along Obvodny Canal to the old clothes market. After bargaining fiercely, she bought a cap with earflaps, and some woolen socks.

In the evenings, sitting there in her unheated, untidy room, she stitched together all sorts of big and little bags, out of old rags. They'd be needed when the time came to make up a parcel. Plywood boxes of various sizes stuck out from under the bed.

She now ate practically nothing—only bread and tea. She wasn't hungry, and anyway, she had no money. The food for the parcels was expensive. She didn't heat her room more often than once a week, for the sake of economy. For that reason, too, she always sat at home in her summer coat and mittens. When she was really cold, she simply got into bed. There was no point in cleaning up her cold room—it was cold and uncomfortable anyway—so Olga Petrovna gave up sweeping the floor, and only flicked the dust off Kolya's books, the radio and the cogwheel.

Lying in bed, she would think about her next letter to Comrade Stalin. Since the time when Kolya was taken away, she had already written three letters to Comrade Stalin. In the first one, she had asked him to review Kolya's case and have him released, since he was not guilty of anything. In the second, she had asked to be informed where he was, so that she might go there and see him just once more before she died. In the third, she implored him to tell her one thing only: was he alive or dead? But there was no answer. . . . The first letter she had simply dropped into the mailbox, the second one she had sent by registered mail; the third one, with a return slip for confirmation of delivery. The return slip came back after a few days. In the column "Signature of recipient" was an incomprehensible scribble, in small letters: *eryan.*

Who was this mysterious "eryan"? And had he given her letter to Comrade Stalin? The envelope had been marked "Personal and private."

Regularly, once every three months, Olga Petrovna went to one of the legal advice bureaus. She found the defense lawyers pleasant to talk to—they were courteous, not like the prosecutors. There was a line there too, but not much of a one, only a matter of an hour or so. Olga Petrovna waited patiently, seated in the narrow corridor, resting her hands and her chin on her cane. But she waited in vain. All the counsels, no matter to whom she would turn, explained to her there was, unfortunately, nothing to be done to help her son. Now if his case had been brought up for trial . . .

Then one day—it was exactly one year, one month and eleven days after Kolya's arrest—Nina Kiparisova appeared in Olga Petrovna's room. She entered without knocking, gasping for breath, and sank down onto a chair. Olga Petrovna looked at her in amazement: Nina Kiparisova was afraid of Boris Ignatyich's case being linked up with Kolya's, and therefore never came to see Olga Petrovna. And now she had suddenly arrived, sat down, and was sitting there.

"They are being released," she said hoarsely, "people are being released. In the line just now—I saw it with my own eyes—a man who'd been released came to get his papers. He wasn't emaciated, only his face was very white. We all crowded around him, asking: 'What was it like there?' 'All right,' he says."

Kiparisova looked at Olga Petrovna. Olga Petrovna looked at Kiparisova.

"Well, I'll go now." Kiparisova got up. "I've got a place reserved for me in the line at the prosecutor's office. Please don't see me off, so that no one sees us in the corridor together."

They were letting people out. Some people were being let out. They were coming out of the iron gates into the street, and returning home. Now they might release Kolya too. The bell would ring—and Kolya would come in. Or no— The bell would ring and the mailman would come in: a telegram from Kolya. After all, Kolya's not here, he's far away. He will send a telegram from somewhere on the way.

Olga Petrovna went out onto the landing and opened the door of the mailbox. Empty. Nothing inside. Olga Petrovna stood for a moment staring at the yellow side of the box—as though she could make her stare produce a letter from this box.

She had barely time to get back to her room and was threading a needle (she was stitching up another bag) when her door again opened without knocking, and the nurse appeared, followed by the house manager.

Olga Petrovna stood up, her back guarding the pile of food.

Neither the nurse nor the house manager said a word of greeting to Olga Petrovna.

"You see!" the nurse immediately rapped out, pointing to the kerosene can and the primus stove. "You just have a look. She's fixed up a whole kitchen here. Soot, filth, she's blackened the whole ceiling with smoke. Breaking down the proper operation of the house. She doesn't want to do her cooking in the kitchen, with the others—been sulking ever since we discovered her systematically stealing the kerosene. Her son's in a camp, exposed as an enemy of the people, she herself is without any fixed occupation, an unreliable element, in short."

"You, citizen Lipatova," said the house manager, turning to Olga Petrovna, "take the cooking equipment into the kitchen immediately. Or else I'll report to the police. . . ."

They went out.

131

Olga Petrovna carried her primus stove, her kerosene can and her pots back to their old place in the kitchen, then lay down on her bed and burst out sobbing.

"I can't stand it any longer," she said aloud, "I can't stand it any longer." And again, in a shrill voice, syllable by syllable, completely unrestrained: "I can-not, I can-not stand it an-y long-er. . . ."

She pronounced the words as convincingly and persistently as if there had been someone standing there in front of her, declaring that, on the contrary, she could easily stand more.

"No, I cannot stand it, it is impossible to stand it any longer!"

The policeman's wife came into her room.

"You mustn't weep . . ." she whispered, wrapping Olga Petrovna up in her blanket. "Just listen a moment to what I am saying. What they're doing is not legal, my husband says: since you've not been deported, that means that no one has any right to touch you. Don't you weep! My husband says a lot of people are being let out now—God willing, Nikolai Fyodorovich will return soon, too. . . . That daughter of hers is getting married soon, so her mama has her eye on your room. But don't you move, that's all. Mama's after it for her daughter, and the house manager's after it for his lady friend. So they'll be fighting over it. . . . But just don't you cry! It's true what I'm telling you."

## SEVENTEEN

In winter, through the double windows, the night street sounds scarcely penetrated into the room; but Olga Petrovna could hear the rustlings and creakings going on in the apartment all night. First, the persistent gnawing of the mice—she only hoped they wouldn't get at the bacon she'd bought for Kolya! Then in the corridor, the creaking of the floorboards and, whenever a truck went by, the rattling of the front door. In the accountant's room, a clock struck solemnly every quarter of an hour.

Kolya would soon come back. That night, Olga Petrovna no longer doubted that Kolya would soon come back. . . . Kiparisova said so, and the policeman Doroshko. . . . He must come back because, if he didn't, she would die. If they were beginning to let out innocent people, then they'd soon let Kolya out, too. It was impossible that they should

133

release other people, and not him. Kolya would come back —and how ashamed the nurse would be then! And the house manager! And Valya! They wouldn't even dare raise their eyes at him. Kolya wouldn't even say good day to them. He'd just look through them, as if they weren't there. When he came back, they'd give him a responsible job somewhere immediately—and even a medal!—in order to make amends for the wrong they'd done him. There'd be a medal on his chest, and he wouldn't even say good day to the nurse or to Valya! . . .

Toward morning Olga Petrovna fell asleep. It was ten o'clock before she woke up.

When she woke up, she remembered: something good had happened yesterday, she'd learned something good about Kolya. Ah yes! They were starting to let people out of prison. And if they were being released, that meant that Kolya too would soon come back. And Alik. All would be well, as before. Olga Petrovna caught herself thinking: then Natasha, too, will come back.

No, Natasha would not come back. . . .

But Kolya—why Kolya was already on his way back, his train was perhaps already pulling into the station.

Returning from the library that afternoon, Olga Petrovna stopped in front of the window of a commission shop and stood before it for a long time. There was a Leica camera on show there. Kolya had always dreamed of a camera. Suppose she sold something and bought Kolya the Leica to celebrate his return! Kolya would soon learn how to take pictures—he always picked everything up so quickly!

All that day Olga Petrovna felt happy and elated. She even felt hungry, for the first time in many days. She sat down in the kitchen to peel potatoes. Supposing she did

134

buy Kolya a camera, there'd be the problem of where he could develop his films. A completely dark room was necessary. Ah! the cubbyhole, of course. There was wood there, but a place could be cleared. She could carry part of her wood, little by little, into her own room, and ask the policeman's wife to take a bundle into hers—she wouldn't refuse—that would make room. Kolya would photograph everyone: Olga Petrovna, the policeman Doroshko and his wife, and their twins, and young ladies he knew—only Valya and her mother he wouldn't photograph on any account. He'd have a whole album full of photographs, but neither Valya nor her mother would ever get into his album.

"D'you still have a lot of wood left in the cubbyhole?" Olga Petrovna asked the policeman's wife who had come into the kitchen for a broom.

"About three bundles," the policeman's wife replied.

"Do you like having your photograph taken? I loved it very much when I was young, by a good photographer, of course. . . . You know what? Kolya's been released."

"You don't say!" exclaimed the policeman's wife, dropping her broom. "So you see! And you were killing yourself!" She kissed Olga Petrovna on both cheeks. "What did he send, a letter or a telegram?"

"A letter. I've just received it . . . registered."

"I didn't hear the mailman come. You can't hear anything with these primuses going."

Olga Petrovna went back to her room and sat down on the couch. She felt she had to sit somewhere quickly, to recover from her own words and grasp their meaning. "Kolya's been released. They've released Kolya. . . ." In the mirror she saw a wrinkled old woman with dirty gray hair streaked with white. Would Kolya recognize her, when

135

he returned? She stared deep into the mirror until everything started swimming in front of her eyes, and she could no longer make out which was the real couch and which the reflection.

"You know, my son's been released. From prison," she said to the woman who worked in the library with her, writing out cards at the same table. Until now, she'd never heard a single word from Olga Petrovna, and Olga Petrovna didn't even know what her name was. But she felt she simply had to repeat her statement like an incantation.

"Well, now!" the woman answered.

She was a fat, untidy woman all covered with hairs and cigarette ash.

"Your son was probably not guilty of anything—and so they released him. People in our country aren't kept in prison when they've done nothing. . . . He was away for a long time, your son?"

"One year and two months."

"Well, they looked into the matter and then released him," said the fat woman, putting down her cigarette, and beginning to write.

That evening the policeman Doroshko bumped into Olga Petrovna in the corridor and congratulated her.

"You'll be throwing a celebration," he said, shaking her hand and smiling broadly. "And when will Nikolai Fyodorovich be coming to see his mother?"

"He'll put in a month or two at the plant, then go to the Crimea for a rest—he needs a rest very badly!—and after that he'll come and see me. Or maybe I'll go and see him," replied Olga Petrovna, amazed herself at the ease with which she was saying all this.

She was happy and excited, she even walked faster. And she wanted to go around telling people all the time,

"Kolya's been released. Did you know? They've released Kolya!" But there was no one to tell.

That evening she went to a shop to buy bread and ran into the polite accountant from the publishing house. Only the day before she would have crossed over to the other side of the street upon seeing him, because everything that reminded her of when she had worked there was painful. But now she smiled at him from afar.

He bowed gallantly, and asked at once:

"Have you heard our news? Timofeyev's been arrested."

"What?" gasped Olga Petrovna. "But he—but it was he who exposed all the saboteurs. . . ."

The accountant shrugged his shoulders.

"And now someone's exposed him. . . ."

"You know, I've had good news," Olga Petrovna hastened to tell him. "My son's been released."

"Ah! Allow me to congratulate you. I didn't even know your son had been arrested."

"Yes, he was, and now he's been released," said Olga Petrovna gaily, saying good-by to the accountant.

Returning home, she automatically looked into the mailbox. No letter. Her heart sank, as it always did at the sight of the empty box. Not a line for a whole year. Surely it must be possible to smuggle out a letter through someone? For a year and two months there had been no news of him at all. Could he be dead? Was he still alive?

She lay down on the bed feeling that she'd never be able to fall asleep. But then she took some Luminal, a double dose. And fell asleep.

## EIGHTEEN

T oday I received another letter," Olga Petrovna told them in the kitchen the next morning. "Imagine, the director of the plant has appointed my son as his assistant. His right hand. The Mestkom has procured him travel orders to the Crimea—there's gorgeous scenery there. I went there in my youth. And when he comes back he's getting married. To a Komsomol girl. Her name's Ludmila—a pretty name, isn't it? I will call her Milochka. She waited a whole year for him, although she had many other proposals. She never believed anything bad about Kolya." Olga Petrovna looked triumphantly at the nurse, standing beside her primus stove. "And now he's going to marry her—at once, as soon as he returns from the Crimea."

139

"That means you'll have grandchildren to fuss over!" The policeman's wife's face was wreathed in smiles.

The nurse didn't even raise an eyebrow. But a moment later, when Olga Petrovna returned to the kitchen after going to her room for some salt, she suddenly said "Good morning" to her, as though she'd just seen her for the first time that day. The first "Good morning" for her in a whole year.

It was Olga Petrovna's day off, and she decided to tidy up her room. Even if Kolya wasn't free yet, he was bound to be freed any moment now. He would arrive, and the room was in such a mess.

Glancing at herself in the mirror, Olga Petrovna decided she simply must start waving her hair again. Otherwise there would be nothing but dank gray strands hanging down.

She pulled out some boxes from under the bed and lit the stove with them. The plywood burned excellently, with a cheerful crackling. Olga Petrovna was deliberating where she could store all those cans so they would not encumber the window sill. And what did she need so many cans for? When she needed them, she could always go and buy some in the store.

She decided to wash the windows and the floor. Her legs were aching as they always did, and she had a pain in the small of her back, but what could she do, other than put up with it? She tore up the bags to use as rags.

While the water was heating, she must go and shake the carpet. Olga Petrovna dragged the carpet out onto the landing. Through the cracks of the mailbox she could see something inside. Olga Petrovna, with an effort, went to get the key.

Inside the box was a letter. A rough pink envelope. She

140

read the inscription: "To Olga Petrovna Lipatova." Her name was written in an unfamiliar hand. And there was no address, no postmark, nothing.

Forgetting the carpet on the landing, Olga Petrovna rushed back to her room. Sat down by the window and tore open the envelope. Who could it be from?

"Dearest Mother!" there was written, in Kolya's hand, and Olga Petrovna was so dazed by the sight of his writing that she lowered the letter onto her knees.

Dearest Mother!

I am alive, and now a kind person has promised to deliver a letter to you. How are you, where is Alik, where is Natalya Sergeyevna? I think of you all the time, my dear ones. It is terrible for me to think that you may now be living somewhere else, not at home. Mother, you are my only hope. My sentence was based on the evidence given by Pashka Gusev—you remember, a boy in my class? Pashka Gusev declared that he had persuaded me to join a terrorist organization. And I had to confess, too. But it is not true. We never had any such organization. Mother dear, the investigator Rudnev beat and kicked me, and now I'm deaf in one ear. I've written many appeals since I've been here, but have never had an answer. You must write yourself, saying you are my old mother, and put the facts before them in your letter. You know yourself that I never even saw Pashka Gusev after I left school, since he studied at a different institute. And even at school I was never friends with him. They must have beaten him badly, too. I embrace you fondly. Greetings to Alik and Natalya Sergeyevna. Mother dear, you must do something quickly, I will not last long here. Fond kisses, from

your son, Kolya

Olga Petrovna threw on her coat, jammed on her hat, and still carrying a dirty rag in her hand rushed off to see

141

Kiparisova. She was afraid she might have forgotten the number of her apartment, and would not be able to find it. She clutched the letter in her pocket. She had left her cane behind, and ran along clutching the walls. She felt her legs giving way under her: no matter how she hurried, Kiparisova's place was still far away.

Finally she entered the building and, with a supreme effort, dragged herself up to the third floor. This must be it. Yes, this was it. "Kiparisova, N. V. Ring once."

The door was opened by a little girl, who immediately turned and ran away. Making her way past the cupboards in the dark corridor, Olga Petrovna pushed open a door at random, and went in.

Kiparisova sat there on a trunk in the middle of the room, in her coat and holding a cane in her hands. The room was completely empty. Not a single chair, or table, not a bed or curtains—only a telephone on the floor near the window. Olga Petrovna sank down on the trunk beside the old woman.

"I am being deported," said Kiparisova, showing no surprise at the appearance of Olga Petrovna, and not even greeting her. "I leave tomorrow morning. I've sold everything and leave tomorrow. My husband has already been deported. For fifteen years. You see, I've already packed. There's no bed, nothing to sleep on, I'll sit up all night on the trunk."

Olga Petrovna handed her Kolya's letter.

Kiparisova sat reading it for a long time. Then she folded the letter and shoved it into the pocket of Olga Petrovna's coat.

"Let's go into the bathroom," she whispered. "There's a telephone here. One can't talk about anything near a telephone. They've inserted some kind of special gadget

142

into the telephone, and now one can't talk about anything—every word you say is heard at the exchange."

Kiparisova led Olga Petrovna into the bathroom, put the hook on the door and sat down on the edge of the tub. Olga Petrovna sat down beside her.

"You've already written the appeal?"

"No."

"Then don't write any!" whispered Kiparisova, bringing her huge eyes, ringed with yellow, close up to Olga Petrovna's face. "Don't write, for the sake of your son. They're not going to pat you on the back for an appeal like that, neither you nor him. And do you imagine you can write that the investigator beat him? You can't even think such a thing, let alone write it. They've forgotten to deport you, but if you write an appeal—they'll remember. And they'll send your son farther away, too. . . . Through whom was this letter sent, anyway? . . . And where are the witnesses? . . . What proof is there?" She looked around the bathroom with wild-looking eyes. "No, for God's sake, don't write anything."

Olga Petrovna disengaged her hand, opened the door and left.

In utter exhaustion, but still hurrying, she made her way home. She felt she had to lock herself in, to sit down and think things over. Should she go to the prosecutor, Tsvetkov? No. To the defense lawyer? No.

She took the letter out of her pocket and threw it down on the table, then removed her coat and sat by the window. It was growing dark and lights were already beginning to go on in the dusk outside. Spring was on the way, how late darkness fell already.

She must decide, she must think it over. But Olga Petrovna sat by the window, thinking of nothing.

"Mother dear, the investigator Rudnev beat me. . . ."

Kolya still wrote his d's with a loop. He always wrote them like that although, when he was small, Olga Petrovna had taught him he must write them with a downward stroke. She had taught him to write herself. In a lined school notebook.

It was now quite dark. Olga Petrovna got up to turn the light on, but simply couldn't find the switch.

Wherever was the switch in this room? She fumbled along the wall, bumping into the furniture which she had moved out of place in order to clean the room.

She found it. And caught sight of the letter immediately. It was lying, creased and crumpled, on the table.

Olga Petrovna took a box of matches out of a drawer. She struck a match and lit a corner of the letter.

The letter burned, the corner curled slowly, coiling up into a tube. It curled up completely and burned her fingers.

Olga Petrovna dropped the flame on the floor and stamped on it.

*19 November 1939–February 1940*